BOY WANTED

BOY WANTED

by JANET LAMBERT

E. P. DUTTON & CO., INC.

NEW YORK.

For Leone

BOY WANTED

"I think everybody should be excused from the first week of school," Ginger Johnston complained, shifting her heavy load of books from one arm to the other and mopping her hot face on a wilted piece of cleansing tissue. "It's just too darned hot!"

The tissue disintegrated in white patches, and as she picked them off, she asked, "Don't you hate it?"

Up to a few minutes ago, Patty Palmer, toiling up the steep hill beside Ginger, hadn't hated it at all. This first real day of school had been exciting. Being a sophomore and knowing her way about had given her a feeling of importance. She had smiled and spoken to at least fifteen boys who were upper classmen, and had exchanged light banter with the ones in her own home room. It had been great fun; and it wasn't until they all disappeared and left her with only Ginger for the long walk home that her spirits had drooped.

"I guess so," she said, wishing Ginger could turn into someone else—a boy. Preferably one with dark eyes and dark hair.

Patty and Ginger considered themselves "best friends." They lived a stone's throw from each other in Cheltham's newest development, in two ranch-type houses exactly

11

alike in floor plan. They were both sophomores, and they had the same interests: school, boys, fun—and Patty. They endlessly discussed the same subjects: dates, parties, clothes —and Patty. And while Ginger always told everyone proudly, "Patty's my best friend," Patty truthfully amended her statement to, "Ginger's my best *girl* friend."

Ginger didn't mind. She had a host of friends of both sexes, but for some strange reason—one that completely baffled her parents—she kept Patty at the top of her list and could hold out for hours in the role of patient listener. She didn't envy Patty, who was the prettiest girl she knew, or try to copy her. Ginger had tan hair that curled softly if she kept it short and remembered to help it along with nightly pin-ups, honest gray eyes with sparse tan lashes, and a short, pert nose. Patty had light foamy curls made with a permanent waving lotion, enormous blue eyes that were more than properly lashed, and other nice features. She even had dimples and feminine curves, instead of Ginger's almost straight-up-and-downness.

"What are you going to do, now?" she asked, when they had reached the top of the hill and it was useless to look back.

"I don't know." Ginger's house was down the first side street, Patty's on the second, so she stopped to rest. "Want to come home with me?" she asked. "Or would you rather go to the Center and dance?"

"The *Center!*" Patty's disdain rose to a shriek. "Why should I want to go *there?*" she cried.

"You always used to. You couldn't wait to hot-foot it to town."

"That was last year. The Center's for babies. Nobody who's fifteen would be caught dead in the place."

"You're fourteen," Ginger answered, parking her books on the sidewalk until she knew which way she was to move. "You've got a whole month to go before you're fifteen, and I've got two. Why rush it?"

"Well, I'm not going to the Center with the crumbs." Patty tossed her blond mane and loved the way she did it. "I suppose," she said with withering scorn, "you're planning to sit on the grass while dumb old Spark Plug works on his antiquated crate and asks you to pass his tools to him."

"Yipes, that's neat." Ginger grinned her appreciation of such an articulate sentence. "Steve's going over to help Spark Plug," she said. "If you'd ever listen, you'd know it."

Spark Plug, christened Elston Howard Blake, was a motor fanatic. His side yard joined Ginger's and was back to back with Patty's. Patty, except for two garages which somewhat blocked her view, could look out any of her back windows and watch a gang in coveralls eat the cake and cookies Ginger supplied them. Ginger's allowance always seemed to end with Spark Plug and his friends.

"There's sure to be a gang of boys there," Ginger tempted.

"Not anybody I'd want to know."

Tim Ford had fooled around at Spark Plug's the year before; and afternoon after afternoon, Patty had sat beside a mess of a car, first on the hard, cold ground, later on jolly little dandelions and eager grass blades, and during the heat of summer, under a sprinkler. Now Tim was back with his parents in Lake Forest, Illinois. After a year at his grandmother's, he was home—right back with the "steady date" Patty had helped him forget. Illinois seemed an endless distance from Pennsylvania.

"I don't want to go to Spark Plug's," she sighed, a lump rising in her throat. "Don't you see I can't *bear* to?"

"Oh, gosh." She was acting like a widow again. Ginger had nursed her through two bereavements, one of which had been Patty's own doing. Steve Harding had been Patty's "solid" until Tim had come along and caused Patty to feel that it would be wise to "divorce" him.

"I'm not like you," Patty pointed out patiently. "I can't go ripping around with just anybody. Knowing someone as fine as Tim has made me particular."

"Umhum, I get it." Ginger had watched Miss Patricia Palmer in action all day. "Then I guess you won't mind if I go," she said. "I'm the grease monkey type, myself."

She picked up her books again, grunting as if lifting the sidewalk with them, but Patty fell into step beside her. "I don't want to go home," Patty said. "It's lonesome."

"Okay." Ginger wasn't surprised. Patty never liked to be alone. She had to have companionship, even if only on the far end of a telephone wire. "Well," she decided, "this is the day Mom goes to her bridge club, so we can make fudge. Mary Lou said she might come by after she goes shopping with her mother. She wants a wool skirt and one of those new middy blouses."

"She'll look awful in it. She's fat."

Patty wrinkled her nose at the thought of Mary Lou Coddington's lumpy figure, and scarcely listened to Ginger say, "But she's cute. She says the cutest things, and she's fun. She's smart, too, and she's vice president of our class."

"Who wants to be that?" Patty secretly had. Class offi-

cers stayed after school for meetings, appointing committees and having a whopping good time. She had hoped
to win that election at the end of the spring term, and
had done everything but actually plead, "Please vote for
me." Mary Lou's victory had saddened her whole last
day of school and it had taken her all summer to convince
herself that being a class officer would mean giving more
hours to dedicated duty than she had to spare. Ginger
had shared that trying time, but she kept still.

So they walked up a flagstone path and into the Johnstons' small neat hall. "Just drop your stuff," Ginger
said, "then we'll go out and see if Mom left a note in the
kitchen for me."

"My hair's a mess. Go on, I'll be there."

Patty took out her comb and did a repair job at a
mirror which hung on the wall in the exact spot one
occupied in her own home. This one was an early American antique, like the small commode below it, while the
Palmers' was in a gold baroque frame and hung above a
marble-top table. Both living rooms were the same size
and shape. The Johnstons liked antiques, the Palmers
liked slip-covered furniture. The Johnstons liked a large
Oriental rug and the Palmers preferred wall-to-wall car-
peting, but Patty could walk through the same arrangement of furniture to a dining-room archway, turn right
at a center table and push open the door to a kitchen
that had a breakfast alcove. Or she could have opened a
closed door in the living room and traversed a long hall
where three bedrooms and two baths were concealed.
Either girl could have walked through either house blind-
folded, but Patty chose to do it with her compact open,
critically studying its reflection of her two red lips.

15

"I'm not sure," she said thoughtfully, sitting down on one of the chairs at the breakfast table and spreading out her full cotton skirt, "if I ought to go on using such a juvenile shade of lipstick."

"Huh?" Ginger, ladling sugar into a pan, wiped her hands on her equally full skirt that showed the effects of a long hot day, and turned around.

"I used this shade all last year," Patty went on, still looking and frowning, "because Bonnie said it was right for me, and Doug would have murdered me in cold blood if I hadn't."

Douglas was Patty's older brother, and Bonnie was his girl. They were going away to college in a few days, and Patty was sure their noose of eternal faithfulness would ravel apart when they separated. The world was too full of unattached girls who were looking for a basketball star, a future journalist who sold his articles, even now, who was six-feet-one and had wavy hair. Douglas had all these assets. Bonnie—Patty wasn't so sure that the male sex would trample a path to Bonnie's dormitory. Bonnie was little and cute, smart, kind, sweet, but she wasn't over-burdened with looks. She had selected the correct pale shade of lipstick for Patty to wear, had taught her how to use it, but she wouldn't be around to constantly tell Douglas that Patty smeared it on too thick.

"They won't be here to fuss about what I do," she went on. "Want to go down to the drugstore with me to buy a new one?"

"Mercy, no." Ginger started grating chocolate onto the sugar, and said over her shoulder, "Your mother and father have eyes."

"Oh, I'll wipe it off before I come home, the way I

used to do before Bonnie got into the act." Patty put the compact away, and scolded, "You always get so serious."

She really admired Bonnie Harbach, and thought she must have a lot of charm to have snagged off Douglas; but she preferred to look like the Patty Palmer she fancied herself to be. Since her personality changed at a minute's notice, she never was quite sure what that was, so lived in delighted wonder. Ginger, who was always Ginger, never rose to such heights.

"You might help a little by handing me the milk," Ginger said, grating faster as she tried to hurry.

Pounding had begun in the yard next door, and she still had to cook, beat, cool, and cut. She hadn't time to walk over and peer out the window, so she said, "Golly, what a racket. Who's out there, anyway?"

"That dumb Bill Templeton, and Steve."

"Isn't Spark Plug there, too?"

"Ummmm. . . ." Patty took the milk from the refrigerator, set it on the counter and went back to look. "He's under the car, I guess. Do you still think he's so crucial and the most?"

"No, but he's kind of a brother to me. His parents and mine are always together and I'm used to him." Ginger set her pan on a burner and knew that Patty was staring critically at however much of Spark Plug she could see.

"He's always so grubby," Patty said. "He never seems to get the grease scrubbed off or his clothes hooked together."

She glanced at the waistband of Ginger's skirt that hadn't held onto the tail of a white blouse, and added, "But I guess that doesn't matter to you."

"Not too much."

17

"He doesn't act like a senior, either. He's a worse kid than Steve."

"He's fun."

"And he doesn't like going to parties, or girls." Patty broke off her list of Spark Plug's faults to sit down again and say with a shrug, "I can't understand what you can see in him—or in any other boy, for that matter—after having known Tim. You had first chance at him before I met him."

"Tim's all right." Ginger dropped a brown blob of liquid into a cup of cold water, rolled it about with her finger, then scooped it out and ate it. "He's gone now, though—*pfft*. Has he written to you?"

"No, not yet." The conversation was moving onto the proper path, the one that led to Patty's storehouse of secret doubt, and she asked, "Do you suppose he'll start going steady again with that girl in Lake Forest?"

"Not when he left here going steady with you."

"But he wasn't!" Patty's big blue eyes opened as wide as they would go. "You know perfectly well we didn't go steady," she said. "We were *friends*. Tim wanted it that way. And I did, too," she added as an afterthought.

"Well, you were about the steadiest friends I've ever seen," Ginger returned, turning off the flame and preparing to beat. "Get me the platter."

"But do you think he'll go steady with—her?"

"I wouldn't know. If he has any sense, he won't." Ginger set her pan in the sink and gripped the handle of her long spoon, then looked up to remind, "His parents sent him here to stay with his grandmother so he'd get over being so goony, and his father threatened to ship him off to military school at the next sign of girl trouble. I'd stop

18

being so gone over him if I were you. Now, grease the platter."

"You know a lot about him, don't you?"

"Sure. Why not?" Ginger retorted equably. "His grandmother is my aunt's best friend."

Patty smeared butter over a white dish and held it over the sink, then leaned an elbow on the counter while she said dreamily, "His hair always made me think of fudge, and I told him so. Why do you think he might not still like me?"

"I didn't say that. But he's there, and you're here, and he's seventeen years old."

"What's being seventeen got to do with it?"

"Well. . . ." Spark Plug had put Ginger in her place, once, by carelessly remarking that older guys didn't care much for younger girls. But Spark Plug, she reflected, was poor reference for anyone seeking knowledge of the average male, so she said, "I just meant that Tim will be as old this year as Doug was last year, and will begin going with an older crowd."

"I guess you're right." It seemed strange to accept words of wisdom from Ginger, even though she was more often right than wrong, but Patty nodded. She preferred thinking that age and distance were keeping her from going steady via the airmail route than that Tim had promptly switched his affection back to another girl her age.

The fudge was ready, and Ginger rattled cutlery in a drawer, looking for a knife, while Patty walked back to the table and stood staring out. "I guess you won't have a chance to go over to Spark Plug's," she said, when activity next door caught her attention. "He's going away with Bill and Steve."

"Where?"

"Now, how would I know?"

Patty moved over for Ginger to look, too, and they watched Spark Plug back the family sedan out of his garage. Parts of an old car's motor lay scattered on the grass, so Ginger said from past experience, "They've probably gone off to buy a bolt or something. They're sure to come back."

"Then let's walk over to my house and see if I got a letter."

Patty's mind was still on her own troubled affairs, and she gave a vast sigh when Ginger suggested, "How about sitting up in the tree house so we can watch for Spark Plug?"

"No! I'll never sit up there again," she declared, her eyes closed and her whole face tight with suffering. "It holds too many memories of Tim. It was 'our place.' "

Ginger had thought it was hers, since she and Spark Plug had built it, squabbling amiably up among the pear blossoms, but she did remember the day that Patty had fallen from its rickety ladder and Tim had helped her up from the hard, cold ground. After that, Tim hadn't tinkered quite so much with Spark Plug's motor. He and Patty had sat high up on the uneven platform, swinging their feet while they became very, very friendly.

"Okay," she said, picking up her platter and offering a sugary square to Patty. "We'll walk over to your house and back. You won't want to stay long, will you?"

"Of course not. Just long enough to see if I got a letter."

"Promise?"

"Promise."

They walked across Ginger's back lawn and a corner of

a neighbor's, then stepped over a low hedge into Patty's yard. Ginger carried the fudge and took only the smaller pieces around the edge for herself. And when they went into the Palmers' kitchen that had a yellow-topped table, instead of a red one like the Johnstons', she set her platter down and followed Patty through the swinging door to the dining room.

Douglas and a blond sprite of a girl were in the living room. They were sitting on the carpet, pasting newspaper clippings into a large scrapbook, and they both looked up. "Hi, punk," Douglas said, and he grinned at Ginger. "How're the teeth?" he asked.

"Swell." It was their usual greeting, because Ginger had worn braces for two long years and had had several operations on molars that couldn't break through the bone structure of her small mouth. Douglas had seen Ginger come to the dinner table unable to eat, and he liked her because she was always so cheerful about it. "I just have a retainer with back clamps, now," she said; and opened her mouth to show him.

"Neat going." Douglas winked at her, then noticed Patty again. "What caused you to give up a social afternoon and come home?" he asked.

Patty bristled. "It's my home, too," she said, promptly defensive, as she so often was with this older brother. And she burst out, "I have a right here. It seems to me that I should be able to come in and go out without you always thinking you have to make some crack about it."

"He's only teasing, honey," Bonnie broke in gently, picking up a clipping and reaching for the tube of paste. "Think how dull it's going to be when you won't have him around."

21

"And how peaceful."

The incoming mail was always laid on the hall table, and Patty wished she could see if an unclaimed envelope still lay there. She waited while Ginger brought in her fudge and sacrificed a goodly portion of it, and was inching aimlessly toward the archway, when Douglas halted her by saying astutely, "You got one. Mom put it in your room."

"Thanks." He knew she was waiting for a letter from Tim, but she wouldn't give him the satisfaction of hearing her ask, "Who's it from?" So she inquired with unusual interest, "Is Mother here?"

"Back in my room, hunting more shirts to sew my name tags in."

"Then I'd better tell her I'm home. I always do, you know."

"She'll pant with joy to hear it." Douglas reached up for another piece of fudge, one of the large center pieces that Ginger had been trying to save, and let Patty start along the corridor before he called, "You won't need to stop off at your room on the way. You just got an ad from *The American Girl.*"

"Oh."

Patty kept on walking. She wanted to strangle Douglas, but it gave her great satisfaction to hear Bonnie scold, "That was mean, Doug. It wasn't kind, at all."

"I'm sorry, punk," Douglas called contritely. And she let him wait for her answer.

"Think nothing of it," she said, wishing she could come up with something more cutting. Then she proceeded along, letting her full skirt swing with each step.

She was sorry to leave Ginger in the living room, with

what was left of Spark Plug's candy growing less and less by the minute, but told herself that it served Ginger right. The fudge had been safely parked in the kitchen, and if Ginger had been foolish enough to run back and get it, she deserved to have it eaten.

"Hello, Mother," she called sweetly. "I'm home."

Chapter 2

Ginger sat at her desk, doing her nightly homework. Her bare feet were hooked over the rung of her chair, and every now and then she reached out for a piece of fudge. Spark Plug hadn't come home that afternoon. Or if he had—and from the looks of his tidied yard, he had been there and gone away again—she had missed him while she waited for Patty. So now she made a bad time pass as pleasantly as possible, by eating the candy she had lovingly cooked for him and doing advanced arithmetic to hit tunes on her record player.

"Telephone for you, honey," her mother opened the door to say. "Patty, of course."

"Huh?"

Ginger looked up, and Mrs. Johnston went over to shut off the blare of music that had reached all the way to the living room, even through Ginger's closed door and the one at the end of the hall. *"Telephone,"* she screamed into sudden silence. And in a lower tone, "Patty. I left the receiver off in the kitchen."

"Thanks." Ginger unwound herself and slapped her book shut. A reprieve! "Have some fudge, Mom, while I'm gone," she invited, knowing that her mother never ate sweets. Then she shot along the hallway, through the living room and around the dining room archway, the breeze she made fanning her father's newspaper as she flew past him.

"Hi-ya," she panted into the receiver as she snatched it up and connected with a chair in the breakfast ell. "What's new?"

"Can you come over?" Patty's voice came from such a great distance that Ginger knew she was lying on her back, on her mother's bed.

"Why?" she asked, making herself comfortable, too, by sliding down on her spine and putting her feet up on the table. "Let's just talk here."

"We can't," Patty answered. "My folks had to go out for a while and Doug's mad at me. They made him stay home until they come back and he wants to go somewhere with Bonnie. They won't let me stay here alone, even though they're going to hurry, but he's mad. So can you come?"

"I'll ask." Ginger cracked the receiver onto the wide window sill and reached the living room archway in record time. "Daddy," she asked, swinging around the white door-casing, her face just above the top of her father's head, "may I go over to Patty's? May I?"

"How much more homework have you?"

"One more problem."

"Finish that and you may."

He was about to resume his reading, but Ginger dropped a kiss on the top of his tan hair that exactly matched hers and flung her arms around his neck. "Thanks, old boy!" she cried joyously. "Don't worry about me getting home. I'll either stay all night or call you to stand on the back steps and watch for me."

And once again on the telephone she said, "I'll be there in fifteen minutes."

"Oke. Hurry." Patty, on her end of the line, was assured of companionship. And since there wouldn't be time to telephone anyone else, she smoothed out the flowered counterpane, scuffed into her well-worn loafers, and went back to the living room to tell Douglas that he was now free to leave.

"Who's coming?" he asked, stretched out on the sofa with a magazine.

"Ginger. I tried Jane and Phyllis but they were going to the movies. So Ginger's coming."

Patty sat down in the wing-backed chair and smiled pleasantly at him, but he only frowned back. "What makes you treat Ginger the way you do?" he asked. "She's always about third choice with you, and yet she gives you the best of everything she has."

"She's so sloppy," Patty answered with a shrug. "And she thinks such stupid things are fun."

"Like what?"

"Oh, like working on Spark Plug's car and playing tennis or ping-pong with just any old body, and she belongs to that silly Girls Who Don't Go Steady club, and—well, she's always so cheerful."

"It sounds to me as if you might be jealous."

"Of *Ginger?*" Patty threw back her head and sent him a tinkling laugh. "Mercy," she said. "Ginger never has any real fun."

Douglas still had a few minutes to spend with Patty until Ginger could arrive and make two in the house; so, since he had been planning to give Patty a short lecture before he went away to college, this seemed to be as good a time as any. He was cross with her for living in such a conceited, self-centered little world; so he said bluntly, "You could learn a lot from Ginger, you know."

But Patty only shrugged. "Ginger's very sweet," she said, "but I certainly wouldn't want to be like her."

"Wouldn't you like to have as many friends as she does?"

"Not the same kind."

"Not even the boys?"

Patty started another shrug, but her shoulders didn't drop into place again, so Douglas knew he had caught her attention. "I wonder if you've ever noticed," he said, looking serious, "that there's always a gang at Ginger's. You can come home, but the gang stays there."

"Not all of them."

"Your solid friend Tim did, as long as Ginger wanted him—but she kept bringing him over to you. Look, Patty." Douglas put down his magazine and sat up, clasping his hands between his knees. "I'm going off to college," he said. "It'll be a new experience for me, and I wish you could get a bang out of it, too. By that, I mean I'd like to have you come up to Brown and show you around. I would if you were different, that is," he added, cutting off her pleased eagerness, "if you weren't so all-fired silly and would act your age. The fellows I'll be knowing wouldn't give you a tumble, not even if I asked them to. The minute you started twinkling your big star sapphires at them and swinging your skirts in that ridiculous walk you've picked up, they'd think you were off your rocker."

Patty turned white around her mouth and clamped her lips together. "I suppose," she said through clenched teeth, "that you'd be happy to invite Ginger."

"Yes, I would. Ginger's just the kind of kid sister I would invite," he said. "She's cute, and she's free without being silly, and so darned straightforward."

"I don't have to sit and listen to you." Patty started to rise with great dignity, but he reached out and pushed her back in the chair.

"Now, wait a minute," he said, "I'm not through. There never was a more honest little kid than you used to be. *Fundamentally* honest, I mean—with yourself, and other people. You were always for the underdog, then. Now you walk all over him. *Why*, Patty? What's got into you? What makes you think you're so superior to all the other kids your age, to Ginger—even to Mom and Dad? What makes you try to run everybody?"

"If you're through criticizing me," Patty said, her head high, feeling sick inside but determined to hit back, "you can stop pointing out all my faults that Bonnie's been pointing out to you. I don't need a psychoanalyst."

"Well, that's a hot one." Douglas had promised his mother to try and get through to Patty, but it seemed that he had used too many approaches. One road in would have been better, the one he had first chosen: boys. Patty wanted the boys to like her.

"Bonnie doesn't point out your faults," he said, feeling his way along slowly. "She sees virtues in you that I can't find. She even thinks you'll grow up to be normal."

Patty made no comment that would serve as a guide-post, so he went on, "I know it wasn't fair to compare you with Ginger, and I'm sorry I did. That kid doesn't deliberately try to make people—especially boys—like her. She doesn't even know she's loaded with personality."

"Ginger is?" Two big round tears rolled out of Patty's

28

eyes and slid down her cheeks. Douglas didn't like her! He liked Ginger better, and he sat there saying so, over and over. "I'm sorry," she said in a weak voice, one that sounded properly strained and should make him sorry. And she let her shoulders slump and her head droop so that the tears fell into her lap. "I'll try harder," she said, punctuating her sentences with little sobs. "I'll go to Scout meetings . . . and not care how I look . . . and I won't coax Mother for—for any new clothes."

"Oh, punk." Douglas had always hated it when Patty cried. She could get the best of him that way, and she knew it. As a little boy, her tears had made him let her be first to ride in his new tin automobile, and, later, he had glued his model airplanes together again without telling his parents she had broken them. Now he found himself consoling, "You've got a lot of good points, too, punk. I shouldn't have lowered the boom on you with such a bang."

"What's good about me?"

Patty looked up with the tears still dripping, and he searched his mind for any trait he could praise. "There's always something," he said. And he suggested, "Why don't you ask yourself? Put your faults in one column and your good qualities in another, and then balance them up and see whether you come out minus or plus."

"I haven't any—plusses to put down."

Patty began to weep again, and he said quickly, "Oh, you know you have. For one thing, you're awfully pretty. You've got a lot of poise for fourteen—and you're pretty."

Patty wanted to remind him of her imminent fifteenth birthday, but she only looked gratefully at him and waited for him to go on. "And then," he said, thinking that selfishness, inconsideration, high-handed intolerance of others tipped the scales against her with a thud, "you always make good marks in school."

He was getting nowhere and would have only failure to report to his mother, so it was with great relief that he heard the front door bang open, and Ginger call, "Hi. I'm here."

Patty was sorry to have the curtain fall on such a dramatic scene. She had the center of the stage now, and was prepared to cry again, convulsively if need be, and to remain sweet and submissive until Douglas left for college in a few days. An invitation to visit Brown University was sure to be forthcoming—to a good little sister—so she would play the role for all it was worth.

"Oh, hello," she answered, stabbing daintily at a wandering tear with the neat handkerchief she took from her pocket.

"I came prepared to spend the night," Ginger said, putting her schoolbooks and a pair of wrinkled pajamas on a chair. And she grinned at Douglas. "My teeth are still fine," she said, clicking them, "so you needn't ask. We had steak tonight, and that terrifies Mom, because she's afraid I'll clamp down on a piece of gristle and cost more money. It's awful," she said, smiling broadly around a sigh, "to have the most expensive teeth in the family. Go on over to Bonnie's. We aren't afraid to stay here alone."

"Thanks, Ginger." Douglas was ashamed to be so glad to escape. He thought of patting Patty's curls as he passed her, then decided to retreat in silence. This unprecedented action might disturb her a little.

But it didn't. As soon as the front door closed behind him, she said, "Do you know what he told me?"

"Hunhuh. Are he and Bonnie going to get married?"

"Of course not. He told me a lot of wonderful things about you and me."

"What kind of things?" Ginger thought Patty had been crying, but she wasn't sure. Patty cried so often, from pleasure, from excitement, and in such an effortless way that no telltale blemishes were ever left. And since she cried whenever it seemed wise to cry, perhaps the handkerchief had only been used in maidenly acknowledgment of Douglas's compliments.

"He said—but come back in my room while I tell you." Patty got up and swayed down the hall with the walk Douglas detested. She supposed Ginger was following along behind her, but it wasn't until she had seated herself in the only upholstered chair that she continued, "He said I'm pretty."

"Well, you are." Ginger took the straight chair at Patty's desk, and nodded. "You knew that before Doug told you."

"And he said you have loads of personality," Patty proclaimed, determined to be fair and let Ginger share in the compliments.

"He did?"

"He said you're simply *oozing* with it."

"Well, that's something new." Ginger stared as if she couldn't believe it. "What am I so personalized about?" she asked.

"He didn't say." Patty thought a moment, then shook her head. She hadn't paid attention to Douglas's praise of Ginger, only to his unkind remarks about herself, so she went on, "Doug wrote all the editorials for the school paper last year, so he ought to know what he's talking about. He said that everybody should keep a sort of account book on himself—listing the minuses and plusses, you know—and I guess he thought we have a lot to list."

"What have I got to list?" Ginger asked. "On both sides, I mean. I can think of a lot of faults, but what have I got on the good side?"

"I don't know. Personality, I guess. Doug said I have lots of plusses to put down."

"Hm." Ginger thought that over for a few seconds, her tan-tipped eyelashes blinking rhythmically, before she broke into Patty's contented musing by saying, "I feel like sort of a stranger. I suppose Douglas does know what he's talking about, but it doesn't seem like it. Let's make a list, the way he said to. Maybe I can think about myself better if I see it in writing."

"All right, pass me a sheet of paper and a pencil."

Ginger tore a sheet from Patty's looseleaf notebook, found the least-chewed pencil in a drawer and went across the room with them. "Thanks," Patty said, "but if you're going to use the desk, you'll have to get me something to write on," so Ginger handed her a magazine.

The room was quiet except for sighs and the swish of erasers. Ginger erased almost as much as she wrote. Her minus column grew rapidly, but her credits remained a smudged blank. *Helpful kindness,* she wrote, and rubbed it out. She had grumbled just this very evening because she'd had to leave her favorite TV program to empty a mess of potato peelings. *Loving.* She rarely made plans for anyone but herself. *Thoughtful.* She erased that, too, just as *generous, neat, orderly, considerate, intelligent,* were rubbed out. Their opposites grew in a long, damaging line, and she was left with nothing but *personality* to offset *selfish, dumb, sloppy,* and *wishy-washy.* In a last valiant effort to find some good in herself, other than what Douglas had found and which she couldn't quite believe, she wrote, *morally decent.* Then, not too sure that she would hunt for the owner of a million dollars, should she find it, or push Spark Plug away, should he ever try to kiss her, she erased that, too.

Patty's erasures were entirely different. Her assets far surpassed her liabilities. In spite of Douglas's criticism, she found herself to be most *generous.* Didn't she always pass along her old dresses to the laundress's daughter? And didn't she buy milkshakes for any friend who had spent her allowance? So she gave herself credit for it. *Helpful.* She always set the table when her mother asked her to. *Kind.* She was devoted to Sam, her cat, and was always *polite, intelligent,* and *loving* to those who loved her. She supposed she was too *intolerant* of those who have no truly high ideals, so she put that down as a debit but switched it over to her assets at the last minute.

"Well," Ginger said, "I guess this is the best I can do. Do you want to read yours first?"

"You do it." Patty laid her paper in her lap while she listened to Ginger's halting recital. "Well, my goodness," she said at the end, "if Doug hadn't found one virtue in you, you wouldn't have any, would you?"

"No, I guess not." Ginger folded the scribbled piece of paper and hid it in her pocket as she asked, "Is yours any better?"

"I have fourteen plusses and one minus," Patty answered, looking down at her list. "I don't see how you could be so all-wrong at your age."

"I am. I only took *personality* because Douglas said to," Ginger answered, somehow dreading to hear Patty rattle off a list of virtues. She couldn't look up during the self-satisfied listing, but at the end she said haltingly, "You have a nice long list of plusses. I guess I'm just personality, and you're plus."

"Hi, Perse," Patty said with a giggle.

"Hi, Plus," Ginger returned, glad for a joke in an embarrassing moment. "That's us—personality plus."

They began to whoop with laughter, each completely satisfied with her half of the title; and Patty said, "Personality and Plus. We can call each other that, but let's never tell what it means. Will you shake on it?"

"Sure."

They stood up and clasped hands, pumping solemnly, until Patty remembered her homework. "Look, Perse," she said, "all this foolishness has wasted my evening. Have you done your math?"

"Umhum. The problems are awfully hard and long."

"Then I'll just copy yours and save time. Shoot 'em over." Patty seated herself at the desk and left Ginger standing uncertainly beside her.

"You won't be able to copy my theme," Ginger said uncomfortably.

"Oh, I've done mine." Patty found her pen and opened her notebook to a smooth, fresh page. "Maybe it'd be better if you read off the figures to me," she said. "After I have them down, you can explain how you got your answer and why, and it won't take so long. Shoot."

34

Chapter 3

The second day of school dragged hotly on. The sophomore class had new home rooms, and the teacher who presided over Ginger's section was as efficient and accurate as an IBM machine. He was also as mechanical. Ginger missed Miss Maxwell's smile and the easy effortless way she kept order. A headshake from Miss Maxwell had been enough to quiet the most unruly, while a cold stare from Mr. Stillman shocked the whole room into numbness.

"I don't like him," Patty said, going home, walking backward again to watch the long line that straggled up the hill behind her. "I can't stand a whole year of his grouchy old puss." Then she swung around and said with a sigh, "This is going to be an awful year. We've got the crummiest bunch of boys in our room—not one you'd even look at. Are we going to the drugstore?"

"I guess so."

"Just to meet Mary Lou and Sally!" Patty said disgustedly. "Jane and Phyllis won't be there because they still go steady."

"They can't go steady in the afternoon," Ginger pointed out, "when Fred and Hal have football practice."

"They sit in the bleachers and wait."

Patty plodded on, still watchful; and when they reached

35

Ginger's corner, she said crossly, "I almost wish I hadn't stopped going steady with Steve. I knew Tim wouldn't be back this year."

"Well, look around and use your plusses." Ginger turned onto her own narrower walk, and when she saw that Patty continued her forward motion, she stopped to ask, "Aren't you coming with me to leave my books?"

"I think I'd better go home first."

"Sure. You might have a letter." Ginger couldn't resist making that last knowing remark, but she grinned and added, "I'll come over and pick you up. 'By, Plus."

" 'By, Perse."

Patty swung lonesomely on, and Ginger skipped along the last half block. Her mother was cutting asters and roses in the side yard, so she laid her books on the front steps and walked across the grass to her. "Hi, Mom," she said. "It's hot, huh?"

"Boiling." Mrs. Johnston straightened up and wiped her damp forehead. She was a pretty woman in her middle thirties, slender, with the healthy glow and lithe coordination of a woman who is good at sports. "Dad's coming home early," she said, "and we're going out to the club for a round of golf before dinner. Have you any plans?"

"Just getting Patty and going to the drugstore for a malt with the kids."

"Which reminds me to tell you something." Mrs. Johnston picked up her basket of fall flowers, and said as they walked toward the house, "Aunt Mag was here last night. She was simply bursting with news."

"I wish I'd been here."

Ginger thoroughly enjoyed her aunt, who was her mother's sister. Margaret Partridge had never married, and she considered herself a farmer. She did own seventy beautiful acres that had a brook running through them, and a delightful old house, set on a knoll. But since she couldn't tell a field of wheat from a field of rye, she shared her profits with a very capable tenant farmer and went off to business in Philadelphia every morning. She was president of a large department store, and her fabulous salary had eased many a burden for the Johnstons.

"She had loads of interesting things to tell, as usual," Ginger's mother went on, when they reached the kitchen. "Want to join me in a lemonade, honey?"

"Please." Ginger took two glasses from a cabinet, opened the refrigerator door while her mother set her basket of flowers on the counter, and asked, "Anything special?"

"Oh, goodness, yes. That's what I wanted to tell you. She said Tim Ford's grandmother called her up yesterday and told her that she's expecting Tim to come back for the winter."

Ginger almost dropped the pitcher of lemonade. *"Really?"* she cried, steadying it. "Why?"

"His father has to go back on that Canadian job—things aren't doing well without him—and his mother wants to go, too, even though she does have to rough it. So, up popped the problem of Tim again."

"Well, what do you know!" Ginger set the glasses on the table and held the pitcher with both hands while she poured lemonade into them. "Will Pam come, too?" she asked eagerly.

She had liked Tim's sister, the few times she had seen her, so was sorry to have her mother shake her head and say, "No, she'll stay in boarding school, just as she did last year. Only Tim is coming."

"Oh, I'll have to tell Patty right away! My goodness," Ginger cried, "she'll be so excited she'll faint and fall down!"

"Wait a minute, honey." Mrs. Johnston picked up one of the glasses of lemonade and looked thoughtfully at it as she said, "Let Tim be the one to break his news to her. He'll write to Patty if he wants her to know ahead of time, and perhaps he has, by now."

"Hunhuh." Ginger shook her head. "He hasn't," she said. "The phone would have rung or Patty'd be over here by now. Is he trying to surprise her?" she asked, sitting down, her big eyes puzzled.

"Well. . . ." Mrs. Johnston hesitated before she said truthfully, "I don't know. Everything I heard had been passed through several conversations, and there was a great deal of talk about a girl in Lake Forest. Someone he was crazy about before he came here last winter, I think."

"I know about her," Ginger interrupted, "but I thought he likes Patty, now."

"He probably does. His grandmother thinks he's a wonderful boy, and she's happy to have him stay with her because she rattles around in her big house alone. But she did say that his parents are making it awfully difficult for her by being so rabid on this going-steady business."

"Who isn't—among you old folks?" Ginger retorted, grinning.

"I know. Well, you haven't given us any trouble," her mother answered, looking almost too pleased, "up to now."

"That's because Spark Plug not only won't go steady— he won't go." Ginger was frankly honest, since her devo-

38

tion to Elston Howard Blake had begun at the age of ten and wasn't reciprocated. "What else did Aunt Mag tattle on Tim?"

"Nothing else. She did say that Tim had asked his grandmother to tell Ginger-cookie hello, and that he'd be coming soon. At least that's the way I got the message."

"Okay, so I can't tell Patty." Ginger sat considering her predicament; and after tilting her glass and taking a large gulp from it, she sighed, "She'll kill me if she finds out."

"Oh, honey, I'm sorry I told you." Ginger looked so pitiful, bunched up on her chair instead of sprawling, as she usually did, that her mother added crossly, "Why don't you buck up, child, and keep a few secrets from Patty? You can't spend the rest of your school days worrying about what Patty thinks."

"I like her." Ginger looked up with complete frankness. "She's my best friend," she said staunchly. "And I guess things hurt her more than they do me. She doesn't know how to shrug them off. You see, she's never had to wear braces on her teeth."

"Oh, baby."

"And she's never been afraid that her mother would die in an operation, or that her father wouldn't get a better job when his firm folded up."

"Those things wouldn't have touched her deeply, honey, don't you see that?"

"Maybe not. But losing Tim sure will."

"Then let's hope she hasn't lost him. It might be that he's a little hesitant about coming back, you know, even embarrassed. He left here in such a blaze of glory, with a lot of parties planned just for him, and all your crowd going to the airport to see him off."

"I know. Well. . . ." Ginger got up and said, "Thanks for the lemonade, Mom. I'd better pick up Patty and go to the drugstore."

The little chat was over; and Mrs. Johnston, who wanted to prolong it or at least be able to look out and see Ginger in the driveway next door, asked, "Aren't you going to feed Spark Plug today?"

"I'd better not. I sort of promised the kids I'd meet them." She started out the door, then paused to look over her shoulder and grin. "Spark Plug's my boy," she said, "but it does him good to diet once in a while. If he comes hanging around, you can tell him that I had something better to do."

"I'll give him a cookie."

"Let him starve."

Ginger went racing along her back yard and jumped Patty's low hedge. Spark Plug and Steve began to wave a white rag tied to a stick, and she flicked them a wave of her hand in return. But when she reached Patty's back steps she heard Steve thudding after her.

"Hey, wait," he panted. "How come you aren't helping us today?"

"You mean, how come I'm not feeding you," she retorted.

"We did hear that you'd made us some fudge yesterday and had waited around. We're sorry we didn't come back."

He looked likable, standing there, wearing a pair of Spark Plug's dirty coveralls. He had light stubby hair and ears that stood out, and his blue eyes were crinkled up in half moons. "Spark Plug said to tell you that you

can ride around the block with us after a while, if you
want to."

"I want to, but I can't." An idea came to Ginger, and
she asked, "How about you taking Patty down to the
drugstore?"

"After the dust-off she gave me? No, thanks. You're
roped, kid, and I'll relay the news to your pal."

He went loping off, his white pennant flapping over his
shoulder, and Ginger wished she could go with him. She
liked Mary Lou and Sally, but, unaccustomed to keeping
secrets from Patty, she was apt to have a hard afternoon.
She wished she had asked her mother when Tim would
be coming. What if she and Patty should walk along the
street and meet him? What if they should look up and
see him standing beside their booth? Ginger wasn't sure
she could pretend to be surprised, and she truly thought
that Patty ought to be prepared.

"I sound like he's Enoch Arden," she scolded herself,
"or a husband who was falsely reported missing in the
war. I do wish Patty hadn't had to be so horribly constant
since he left. Oh, dear." And as she pushed open the
dining-room door, she tried to sing out cheerily, "Hi, are
you ready?"

"I'm not going."

Patty sat on the divan in a bower of slip-cover roses,
and Ginger's heart did a flip-flop. Patty had on a fresh
cotton dress and her new patent leather pumps. She knows!
Ginger thought thankfully. And before she could stop
herself, she asked, "Has Tim come?"

"Bonnie's cousin is coming over from Mount Airy,"
Patty went on, talking right over Tim's name and not

41

hearing it. "Doug and Bonnie are always after me to have dates with him, so they're bringing him over."

"Oh, that's *swell!*" Ginger tried to cover her unfortunate slip with a broad, bright smile. "Thank goodness!" she cried heartily. "Now you've got someone to have dates with."

"He's very rich," Patty answered. "He likes going to parties and—and spending money." Then she slumped. Her blue eyes clouded, and she sighed, "He's ugly."

"Well, gee whiz, looks aren't everything." Ginger thought about Spark Plug, who had the kind of face a small child might draw: almost square, with features put in any old place, and spikes of hair scratched blackly above it. "If he's nice and you like him. . . ."

"I don't know him." Patty sighed and looked unhappy, but she said, as if telling herself a few facts, "I have to have *somebody* to take me places. The boys you know won't ask me—now."

"You don't like the boys I know," Ginger pointed out.

"Not after knowing Tim."

Another sigh fluttered through the air, and made Ginger ask quickly, "What's this character's name?"

"Phil," Patty recited. "Phillip Lebensdorfer. He's Pennsylvania Dutch, I guess—like Bonnie's family." Then she added more briskly, "I expect you'd better go before he gets here. I wouldn't want him to think we've been talking him over."

Ginger was glad to leave. She wouldn't have to go to the drugstore, now, because Mary Lou and Sally would have each other. And she wouldn't have to explain to Patty why she had asked, "Has Tim come?" Patty had a way of bringing up something you hadn't known she had

42

heard. "Call me when you come home," she said.

"Oh, I will."

Patty was lost in gloomy thought, so Ginger went happily back the way she had come. Spark Plug and Steve were working over the old car's wheels, now, and she watched them while she walked toward them.

The ancient automobile was a 1914 Overland touring car, complete with side curtains that had lain for years under its back seat. It was so old that it had become valuable, and Spark Plug, to his constant joy and amazement, had acquired it in a most unusual way.

A farmer, who was a friend of his grandfather, had bought it years ago for his only son. Then the son had gone off to the First World War and had never come back. The father couldn't bear to sell the car, or to drive it himself, so he had had it put in one of his big barns and walls built around it.

The walls were made of boards and chicken wire, and from the time he was a small boy, Spark Plug had spent many hours standing outside them, looking in at the car. At first, he had come with his grandfather, later he had pedaled out on his bicycle, and for the last year, he had driven out in his own old wreck. Because he had been so faithful, and because Mr. Green's grief had dimmed during the years, Spark Plug had been entrusted with a key to the padlocked door, and had kept the car shiningly clean. Then Mr. Green died.

"Dad always wanted you to have the car," his daughter said, when Spark Plug went out to say how sorry he was, "but he couldn't bear to see you take it away. It says in his will you're to have it—and do whatever you want to with it."

So Spark Plug had found four tires to fit the valuable old relic he had named "Beauty" when he was eight years old, and had paid a man to tow it home. He was in debt, now, up to the top of his brush of black hair, but he loved Beauty more than anything he owned, or might ever own.

"Come here, Ginger," he called, so upside down that she wondered how he had seen her approach. "Get in and start up the old girl for me."

"Me?" Ginger had never sat behind Beauty's wheel. The nearest she had ever been to the kingly spot was to stand on the running board, watching Spark Plug replace old wiring.

"We have to test the brakes. Well, hurry. Get in." Spark Plug straightened up. His face was streaked with grease, and he wiped it on a dirty rag while he opened the front door. "You know what to do," he said, boosting her over the running board because he was in a hurry. "Pull the gas throttle up about half an inch, and leave it there. That's the gas throttle, there on the wheel, stupid. Move it."

"Okay." Ginger slid a brass lever a little way along a semicircular bar, and waited for more instructions. "Beauty's out of gear," she said, experimentally wiggling the long gearshift beside her, as she had seen him do.

"Tramp down on the starter."

Ginger tramped, and Beauty responded with a roar and a backward shower of sparks from her new exhaust pipe. All her cylinders exploded spasmodically, then gulped and followed each other in rhythm.

"Okay," Spark Plug shouted. "Cut her as low as you can, now."

44

"I am," Ginger shouted back. "My heart's pounding louder than Beauty."

"Think you could steer her?"

"Oh, sure."

"Then this is what I want you to do. Now, listen." Spark Plug leaned over the door and instructed carefully, "I want you to put in your clutch—that's the left foot-pedal—so you can throw her into gear. That's good. Now pull straight back on the shift. Got it?"

Ginger nodded and settled herself to be ready for the next step; and he went on, "Let out your clutch and move a few feet. When she gets rolling, press in your clutch again, and slam your foot brake down. Remember to do both feet at the same time. I've put in new brake linings, and Steve and I'll walk along and check them. Both feet at once—think you can do it?"

"Oh, I guess so. Let me rehearse a minute."

Ginger practiced with her pedals and levers, her tongue between her teeth, while he waited. Never had he accorded her such an honor; and while she knew it was only because not enough of his male mechanics had shown up, she resolved to make him proud of her. "I'm ready," she said, praying that Beauty wouldn't stop her rackety shaking when she started her off.

"Show me."

He stepped back to watch Ginger push with her left foot and pull with her right hand, and Beauty, bless her, move forward.

"Brake!" he yelled. And Ginger trod down with both feet. "Okay. Take her along the driveway."

It was proud progress, if halting. Start—go—stop. Start—go—stop. Eventually, Ginger reached the street, and, hearing no orders to forfeit her post, prepared to press on. The way was clear in both directions. Then, as she turned the wheel, a neighbor's fox terrier, intent on business of his own, trotted straight across her path. In sudden fright and indecision, only one of her feet pressed down. It was the wrong foot. Beauty, braked while still in gear, lurched, coughed, and died.

Ginger gasped with her. She had been so proud and doing so well. Now the two who had been crawling along and working with wrenches, stood up to glare at her.

"It—my foot—the dog. . . ." she tried to explain, making wild gestures at the terrier that was running for cover as fast as he could. And for some strange reason, Spark Plug nodded agreement.

"Start her up again and head her along the street to the left," he said, exactly as if she knew what to do. And he went back again to his work.

Starter. Clutch. Gear. Ginger did each step in turn. "They made you cars tough in the olden days," she told Beauty, turning the big wooden wheel and continuing her spasmodic march.

The roadway was narrow but untraveled, and she wondered what she would do when she reached the horseshoe curve at the end and headed back along Patty's block. She thought she could manage the half circle, if no car or delivery truck loomed up before her, and began to hope that Spark Plug would let her drive all the way past the Palmer residence. For Patty to walk out of the house at the right moment would be more than her brimming cup would hold, but she gripped the wheel with hot, ready hands. She was rolling for longer intervals, now, and stopping only at a command.

And there actually was a car standing at Patty's curb. There wasn't much room to pass by it, either, as it was pulling out and moving toward her. Panic struck again. "Spark Plug!" she screamed. "Help me!" and he appeared beside her.

"Just take it easy," he said simply, not even touching the wheel. "Turn out just a little. 'Atta girl. You'd better put your hand throttle to zero and let Beauty roll along on her own. That's fine."

Beauty was barely moving now, so Ginger risked flinging her hand out to wave. She could recognize Patty on the back seat beside a blur of a boy, and was sure that Douglas, behind the wheel, stared long and hard before he returned her greeting.

"Move over and let me turn her around," Spark Plug said into her joy, when they had rolled almost to the intersecting highway. "You can take over again, if you want to."

Ginger was unable to either accept or decline. She scrambled over to the other side of the seat, breathing hard from the wonder of it all and from swinging her legs across the brake and gearshift in time for Spark Plug to climb over the door and take the wheel. Waves of exaltation washed over her like the surf rolling up on the shore of a beach, and she thought she would drown in them. She knew that Steve climbed in behind her, she saw Patty's house go by again, but when Spark Plug asked, "Want to take her again?" she could only stare through Beauty's high, straight windshield and silently shake her head.

Spark Plug had more than repaid her for all the candy, cake, and cookies she had fed him. He had let her drive!

Here she sat, right on the front seat instead of on the back bumper, and she wanted to give in return. "Mom baked some cookies," she finally managed to say.

"I've got some candy bars in the tool box." Spark Plug swung Beauty into her own driveway and set her down with a jerk. "Her brakes are okay, Steve," he said. "Let's get her emergency working."

He swung himself out, and Ginger opened her door for a more ladylike exit. She was sure she was dismissed for the day, but even stepping so stylishly down was something she had never done before. Then Spark Plug gave her another gift by saying, "You can sit there and pull on the brake when I tell you to." And he asked with a thoughtfulness quite unlike him, "You weren't going anywhere in particular, were you?"

"Oh, no." Ginger came to and found words. "I haven't a single thing to do," she said, "not if you need me."

"I wouldn't call it exactly that," he answered, taking a wad of waste from his pocket and wiping off the wheel. "But we can use you. Get in again."

It was a wonderful afternoon. Ginger sat in the car, quite alone, pulling on the hand brake and easing it off when Spark Plug told her to. Sometimes there would be long intervals when she could hang over the door, listening to grunts and groans beneath her. Rusted bolts are stubborn things, so Spark Plug and Steve banged away without talking much to each other—and not at all to her. Then Spark Plug crawled out to loosen something at her feet, and took the whole shaft out.

"There she is," he said, assembling his rods and wires on the grass. "You can get out now, Ginger."

Ginger dismounted slowly. This had been the best afternoon she had had for a long time, and she wanted it to go on and on. Spark Plug had accepted her as one of his gang again, and she wanted to tell him how grateful she was. Things were as they had been that wonderful spring when they had built the tree house and he had bought his first car. He hadn't owned Beauty and become so popular, then.

"Oh, thank you for letting me drive," she said, knowing she really should go home to set the table for dinner. "It was fun!"

"Fade out." A broad grin took the sting out of his answer, and he patted her thin shoulder with his dirty paw. "You're a good kid," he said, and returned to his work.

Chapter 4

"It was colossal, oh, Mom, it was super!" Ginger proclaimed proudly, rattling silver into place on the dining-room table. She had propped the kitchen door open so she could give her mother a complete account of her triumphant tour. "There I sat—driving. *Actually driving!* And Spark Plug was so pleasant and kind to me. He didn't yell at me once."

Ginger's parents, and Spark Plug's, too, had long felt that Spark Plug should show more good will toward this girl child who tagged happily after him. Both couples agreed that, though she might be a nuisance at times, her devotion had its practical side. Spark Plug's mother disliked baking and Ginger's was glad to know where her daughter spent her afternoons, without having to resort to the telephone. The fathers thought she looked cute in over-sized coveralls.

"I never have been so proud," Ginger caroled, wishing her father would come out of the shower so she could tell him, too. "Imagine! *Me* driving *Beauty!* Oh, I do hope I'll get to do it again tomorrow. Golly." She came to lean against the doorframe and say, with a sudden change of mood, "I'm going to miss Spark Plug when he goes off to college next year. He's not much to look at, so I'm glad he isn't keen on girls. I'd just hate any girl who might turn him down on a date and hurt his feelings. Sometimes I want to slap Patty."

"Why, honey?" Mrs. Johnston put lamb chops in to broil and waited expectantly.

"Because she makes fun of him. She says he always has grease under his fingernails, and dances like a bear in a circus. He does. But my goodness, Mom, he's only interested in being a civil engineer. Someday he'll meet a girl who'll make him want to dress up." Ginger sighed and said unhappily, "I'll bet she'll be a silly sort of girl. I wish I could pick out the right kind for him. Someone with a mechanical mind."

"It seldom works that way," her mother answered. "Doctors seldom have doctor wives, and professional men rarely marry professional women. Opposites attract, you know."

"You mean he might get a fluff-head?"

"He might not marry at all—being Spark Plug."

"That's a thought." The telephone rang, and, skidding over to answer it, Ginger exclaimed, "I hope it's Patty! You know, I've been so busy having fun that I forgot she'd gone off on a date. Just let the table go, Mom, and I'll cut her short and finish it." And she lifted the receiver and said, "Hello."

"Hi, Ginger-cookie." The voice was masculine and so unexpected that she fell onto a chair.

"Oh, mercy, Tim," was all she could think of to answer. And she had to rally her wits to ask, "When did you get here?"

"A couple of hours ago. I called your house but no one answered."

"We weren't home. Well—hello. Welcome back. My goodness." Ginger's eyes sought her mother for advice, and she covered the mouthpiece to whisper, "Shall I ask if he's called Patty?" But Tim's voice was going on and she had to listen.

"How about me coming over this evening?" it was saying. "I haven't any studying to do yet, so I'll watch you suffer."

"Tonight?" Honor was honor. She had an important question to ask before she could make a decision, so she inquired bluntly, "Have you called Patty yet?"

"Why should I?"

"Well, because—well—my goodness!" Her sentence hung there. It was caught on a limb of inadequacy, and Tim had to unhook it.

"Listen, Ginger-cookie," he said, "there's nothing in my book that says I have to call Patty—or that I had to call you. I *wanted* to call you. Get it? There's something I want to talk to you about."

"What?" Curiosity ripped loyalty straight up the middle. Ginger felt she wasn't being fair to Patty, but it seemed important to hear what Tim had to tell her. It might be about that girl in Lake Forest and she could pass the information on to Patty. "Wait," she said, before he could rally to a satisfactory reply. "Don't bother to tell me now. You can come over after dinner. I'll fix it somehow."

She meant that she would fix it with Patty, since they always spent a good part of their evening on the telephone; and when she had hung up, she groaned, "Oh, golly. Now look at the mess I'm in!"

Her father had come in, refreshed from his shower and

comfortably dressed for a warm fall evening, and he smoothed down his wet hair as he stood watching her.

"Gee, Daddy," Ginger said forlornly, forgetting all about her glorious afternoon. "What do you do when another girl's solid says he has something to talk to you about?"

"You listen, I'd say," Stuart Johnston advised, feeling judicial. "Of course, you have to consider the pros and cons of the case."

"There are lots of cons and mighty few pros." Ginger managed a feeble smile as she recited, "Con number one: Patty'll never speak to me again. Con number two: I don't want to get in the middle of something. Con number three: I'm no good at giving advice."

"And the pros?"

"None that I can think of right now." She still had the dinner table to finish, but she waited to ask, "Do you think it's all right to let Tim come over?"

"Now, why would you ask me that silly question?" Her father spoke in such a solemn voice that she couldn't be sure he was teasing. "Patty isn't engaged to the guy, is she?"

"Of course, she isn't. But—well, she did think they were sort of going steady."

"And it seems that Tim didn't. Look here, chick." He went over to tilt up her chin and scold in his quiet way that always made good sense, "Stop worrying. Roll with the punches—play it by ear. You can't make Tim or Patty over."

"I guess not."

"Then stop banging your head against a stone wall.

Your mother and I don't like to see you look so glum. You're our favorite child."

"I'm your only one," Ginger reminded.

"But we still like you best. Now, scoot."

Ginger hustled back to the dining room, and he went over to stand beside his wife at the sink. "Why the dickens, Kathy," he grumbled, "do you let Ginger run her life to suit Patty?"

"I can't help it."

"It's 'Patty says, Patty does,' from morning till night. "Why, Ginger would even give her the proverbial shirt off her back if Patty demanded it. And I'll bet she'd even hand over Spark Plug."

"He isn't hers to give." Mrs. Johnston laughed and passed him a stalk of celery to munch on. "Patty isn't as selfish as she sounds," she went on. "It's just that Ginger has to learn to stand up for herself. She will."

"When?"

"Tonight for a starter. She's getting braver if she lets Tim come over here first." She pushed his hand away from the rest of the celery, so he rubbed his cheek across the top of her head.

"You know, I kind of like you, Mrs. Johnston," he said. "You're smart. I'm awfully glad I didn't marry that little blue-eyed blonde I was so crazy about in the third grade."

"I'm glad you didn't, too. Now please take in the platter of chops and send our daughter out to help me."

Ginger had unusual spells of silence during the meal. Her parents watched her with amused tenderness, and when she slid her chair back from the table and said, "I don't think I care for any dessert," they winked slyly at each other. "I suppose I ought to comb my hair again if

Tim's coming," she sighed. "My dress is all right, but I ought to comb my hair."

"I certainly would," her mother replied, "and I'd put on something less wrinkled."

"He won't notice me too much in the dark. I plan to be sitting on the front steps when he comes," Ginger explained. "If Patty calls me, you can say I'm outdoors somewhere and will call her back. You'll be telling the truth, you know, and the whole thing won't look so *arranged*. I think I can keep Patty from getting mad if I make it seem like an accident."

She took her comb from her purse in the hall and ran it through her hair, studying her face in the mirror. "Patty wouldn't ever have any reason to be jealous of me," she silently told her reflection. "My face is too skimpy and my eyes are too big. I don't know why Doug told her that I have personality—I can't see any."

She went out to take her place on the brick steps with no feeling of excitement. In fact, her heart sank lower and lower, and when Tim parked his grandmother's car in the driveway, she had to take a deep breath to be sure her lungs were working. She also took a quick glance up and down the street and wished he had arrived less ostentatiously—on his own two feet. Patty could see the Johnstons' driveway from her bedroom window, even in the dusk.

"Hi," she said, as he came across the lawn to her, exactly as if he had been gone two hours instead of two weeks.

"Hi, yourself, Ginger-cookie," he returned, dropping down beside her.

He really was good-looking, she thought, with his

smooth hair that Patty had likened to fudge, his lean tanned cheeks, his well-shaped head, his forearms muscularly brown below the sleeves of a white sport shirt. Yet when he sat down and tossed his jacket on the steps beside him, she wondered why she preferred Spark Plug's irregular features. But she was glad to see Tim, in a sisterly sort of way.

"You're getting me into a mess of trouble, you lug," she said. "You could at least have called up Patty, along with the rest of the gang, just to tell everybody hello and be friendly."

"You're the first friend I had here. My grandmother piloted me straight to your house and introduced me."

"And I've had you hung onto me ever since."

"Don't you like me?" he asked.

"Sure I do. I think you're terrific." Ginger hugged her knees and studied him. "But you're an awful lot of trouble," she tacked on. "How am I going to walk to school with Patty tomorrow and not tell her I've seen you? How am I going to look surprised when you loom up in the hall, or somewhere?"

"Do you have to?" he asked, leaning sideways against the jutting white wall of the house so he could face her. "Why can't you just casually mention that Terrible Tim is back again? I didn't go steady with Patty."

"Yes, you did. You called it by a very high-sounding name—friendship—but you two were always together. Who else did you ever take to parties?"

"You," he answered promptly.

"Just to the first one, and on a hay ride. After that, you took Patty."

"Maybe you have a point there." He waited a few seconds before he said gloomily, "It was a big mistake, wasn't it?"

"It was, if you didn't mean it. I suppose you've got yourself attached to Babs Whatever-her-name-is again."

"Not exactly." He was silent for a few moments, studying the signet ring he wore, flipping it back and forth on his finger and watching the gold glisten in the light from a street lamp, before he said, "She's making a play for the Academy boys."

"I'm sorry, Tim."

"I'm not." He looked up then. "I could have stayed home and gone to the Academy," he said. "Dad gave me my choice. I decided I liked the gang here. I can graduate in Spark Plug's class this year if I carry an extra subject. So—I came back."

"I'm glad."

"Spark Plug, and Bill, and Peewee, are top guys, but there's just one hitch."

"What?" Ginger was sure she knew but she thought it was better for him to say it.

"I don't want to be even halfway hooked," he answered, reducing his independent attitude by admitting that Patty had a right to feel some small proprietary interest in him. "I know I sort of moved in last year, but I didn't intend to. I really didn't."

"Well, you did; and Patty," Ginger answered thoughtfully, "is the one you should be telling all this to, instead of me." She knew of another case where the boy had tired of going steady with a friend of Bonnie's and had slithered out of the whole thing in what all the parents characterized as a "disgraceful manner." And she said again, "You ought to tell Patty how you feel, Tim."

"I can't." Tim looked out at the few late moths circling around the street light, which was a big, bright sun in the darkness of their brief lives, drawing them nearer and nearer to its scorching heat. "You know Patty," he said, feeling as helpless as the moths. "You know what a storm she kicked up because Steve Harding got sick and she couldn't go on the hay ride. Just a hay ride! Gosh, Gingercookie, I haven't got the nerve."

"I guess you think I have."

"I hoped so." Tim answered her flat statement with praise that came straight from his heart. "When I knew I was coming back, I told myself you'd help me. You're such a good little friend to everybody, Ginger, and I hoped you could—well, I hoped you could prepare Patty for having me join on again as just one of the gang."

"Oh, murder." Ginger closed her eyes and rested her head in her hands. "What else did you plan to do?" she asked, wanting to have it all over at once. "How did you think you were going to stop taking Patty to parties, or spending your afternoons with her when you came to Spark Plug's?"

"I—I thought. . . ." He hesitated, looking at her silhouette beside him, and finally he blurted out, "Oh, nuts! I haven't given Patty one single reason to believe that we're solid with each other."

"Except to always be around and to take her everywhere."

"It was one of those things. Look, Ginger-cookie." He turned to her and took her hands down from her tousled hair that she had combed so carefully. "I'm counting on you," he pleaded.

"Ha-ha."

"I like you best of all the girls I know, and I have more fun with you. I realized that when I was home, so how about letting me take you to all the parties?"

"No thanks." This was another version of the going-steady business, and Ginger had herself to think of. She had enough trouble managing her own affairs. "I'm not about to get linked with you," she said. "I'll help you all I can, and I'll even go over with you to see Patty right now, before I change my mind and things get worse, but I won't let you shove me into her place. You see," she said, smoothing down her skirt and wondering how he had stayed so neat and cool through such a fracas, "I like Patty. I like you, too, and it's awfully flattering to have you sit out here and tell me your troubles, but I think you've got yourself in a good state of jitters. Patty's not going to hit you, and you don't have to latch onto me for protection."

"I'd like to go back to being the way we were when I first came, Ginger-cookie."

"That suits me fine." Ginger skipped the meaning in his words. "Do you want to go over to Patty's now?" she asked. "You can't just fluff her off, Tim."

"Okay." Tim stood up and reached out to pull her to her feet, as Mrs. Johnston snapped on the hall light and opened the screen door.

"Hello, Tim," she said, "it's nice to have you back." And she went on hurriedly, "Patty's on the phone. It's the third time she's called, so what shall I tell her?"

"Tell her that a tramp dropped by, in the shape of Tim Ford, and that we're coming right over. No, wait, I'll do it myself."

Ginger ran inside to her mother's room and picked up

the receiver. This was one time when she couldn't sprawl comfortably on her mother's bed, but had to sit straight up on the edge. "Guess what?" she said. "That crazy Tim Ford's back in town. He's planning to go to school here."

Only a gasp answered her. It sounded strangled, so she hurried on, "He dropped by here, and we were just starting for your house. Plus?"

"Yes."

Patty's voice was empty. The one little monosyllable made Ginger think of an empty box, and she could almost see Patty packing her pride away in it. "Listen, Plus," she said, praying for the right words to come to her, "he stopped by here first. He thinks of me as a second cousin or something, and he's sort of afraid that you thought you two were going steady. I told him you didn't."

Wherever she was, Ginger knew that Patty was sitting straight up, too. "I told him you're always saying you're only friends," she said. And she suddenly asked, "How was your date?"

"He was—stupid."

The answer was disappointing. Patty could, at the very least, have saved a shred of her dignity to wear, but Ginger went on, "That's too bad. Anyway, we're coming over. If *you* think you're just friends, and Tim thinks you're friends, it won't be so hard to *be* friends."

"I don't want to see him. And I don't want to see you, either," Patty snapped. "You're being two-faced and gloating."

"I'm not." Ginger was annoyed at being made the base of a triangle whose two sides had pulled apart and left her to hold them up. "I'm doing the best I can, Patty," she said crossly. "I had a wonderful afternoon, and I'd like

60

to talk about that and not about Tim. I don't want Tim, and I don't want to drag over to your house with him. My goodness," she said, hoping to shock the desolate soul on the other end of the line into action, "I should think you'd *pretend* a little. I would. I'd say, 'Well, what do you know! Come on over and we'll make fudge,' or something."

She had used the wrong word. She knew it the minute it slipped through her lips. Fudge. Patty and Tim had discovered each other over a pan of fudge. Patty had carried a box of it to the airport. And then there was his hair to remember. "Oh, buck up," Ginger scolded into silence. "I should think you'd count up all your plusses and start using them. Honestly, Patty, I'm ashamed of you. Plus Palmer—the girl with the most! Do you want us to come over, or not?"

"Tim can come," Patty sniffled, her pride stiffened by Ginger's derisive flattery, "but I don't want you spreading your personality around."

That made Ginger laugh. She laughed wholeheartedly and at herself, as much as at Patty, and she said at the end, "I haven't a bit and you know it."

"Doug and Tim think so."

"Oh, Doug's crazy. Tim's using me for a crutch; so what do I do—come or stay home?"

Patty thought she could win Tim back if Ginger kept out of the picture, talking nonsense and hopping about the room. Ginger had got to him first, that was all. Ginger, she told herself angrily, was being deceitful; she was gloating over the role of intermediary. "If Tim cares to come over," she said haughtily, "I'd be glad to see him."

"And I can't come, is that it?"

61

A receiver slammed down and she was left with sudden silence. "Oh, Patty, Patty," she whispered into the empty room, "I know you're hurt and mad, but please don't be mad at *me*. I couldn't help it." Then she got up and went back to the steps.

"Patty thought it would be nice if you'd drop by," she said to Tim, who was still chatting with her mother.

"Aren't you going with me?"

Both Tim and Ginger's mother could see her strained, unhappy face. She looked forlorn, standing in the pool of light; and when she shook her head, Tim said with quick understanding, "Okay. I'll hop over there for a minute, then I'll go on to Spark Plug's—and if you're a good girl and get your homework done, I'll pick you up and we'll charge in to see Mary Lou and as many of the gang as we can make in an evening."

"Will you—will we take Patty with us?" Ginger asked.

"Some other time. Be seeing you later."

He went leaping off the steps and Ginger bent her head. "Oh, Mom," she said, "Patty's mad at me."

"Honey, she'll get over it." Mrs. Johnston put her arms around Ginger's narrow shoulders and drew her close. "These things happen, baby," she comforted. "All girls have quarrels, all boys fight it out with their fists. The same thing happens between countries, darling, and we call it war. It's something we have to understand and accept, Ginger."

"But not with Patty, Mom." Ginger looked up, her eyes clear and earnest as she pleaded, "You don't think she'll stay mad at me, do you? You don't think she'll go on believing that I'm trying to snag off Tim? I'm not, Mom. I don't want to go steady with anybody, and I don't want to be crooked."

"She'll wake up, honey. If Patty has any sense—and, child, she has a lot more of one kind than you have—she'll remember that you're Spark Plug's willing little slave. She'll even remember that you were the one who turned Tim over to her in the first place and that he's much safer with you around than with any of the other girls."

"But what if she doesn't?"

"Ginger, please stop it!" Mrs. Johnston admired her daughter's loyalty, but she thought it should end somewhere. It couldn't go on and on, like eternity. "Listen, darling," she said, feeling inadequate because she didn't know how to make Ginger understand that, "run do your homework. Tomorrow is always a brighter day."

"Oh, Mom." Ginger nuzzled against her mother's shoulder and said into it, "I wish I could be as smart and sure as you are."

Chapter 5

Tim punched the bell beside the Palmers' front door and was surprised to see Mrs. Palmer come through the hall.

"Why, hello, Tim," she said, opening the screen door. "I didn't expect to see you. Have you come back to stay?"

"For another winter," he answered. "My parents are going back to Canada, so here I am. I didn't want to miss any more school than I had to."

He wondered where Patty was; and Mrs. Palmer must have wondered, too, for she took him into the empty living room and said vaguely, "I thought Patty was in here. She was, just a few minutes ago. Mr. Palmer and I are putting the finishing touches on our new basement room, and I came up for more coffee. Patty?" she called, opening the door to the corridor.

"Yes, Mother." Patty's voice came from her bedroom, and it said, "I'm getting some history notes I need. Do you want me, Mother?"

"Tim Ford is here," Mrs. Palmer announced, moving a little to one side so she wouldn't be knocked off balance by Patty's flying figure.

But Patty only answered coolly, "That's nice. I'll be there as soon as I find my notes."

"She's coming," Mrs. Palmer turned back to say, puzzled, but sensing that Patty either wasn't eager to see Tim or was letting him wait for reasons of her own. She hoped it was a bit of each, and her eyes twinkled as she said, "She's coming, so I'd better get back to my work before my boss fires me."

Tim liked Mrs. Palmer. She was so pretty and such a lot of fun. He was sure he could tell her how he felt about going steady with her daughter and she would understand. In fact, he thought it would make her very happy.

"Patty'll be right in," she said. "It's nice to have you back, Tim." And she whisked away.

Tim was tempted to go with her. He had hoped to find the living room full of family when he and Patty greeted each other, because the meeting was bound to be strained. Patty wasn't one to quickly forgive a two-weeks silence and a delayed reappearance, and she knew by now that he was here only because Ginger had sent him. Oh, heck, he thought despairingly, shifting his position for the third time, why didn't I write to her and tell her I was coming? Why didn't I hop right over here when I landed? Why didn't I just let things ride the way they were?

He heard her feet tapping along the hall carpet and summoned a feeble smile. "Hello, Patty," he said, moving uncertainly nearer as she came through the door. "Are you surprised to have me come back?"

"I don't think so." Patty considered him carefully. He hadn't changed at all in two weeks, but then how could he? The time hadn't been as long for him as for her. "It was nice of you to come over so soon," she said. "Are you making the rounds?"

"I'm catching a few," he answered. "You, and Ginger,

65

and Spark Plug, and maybe a couple of others. How've you been?"

"Just fine. School's awfully hot, though."

Patty walked over to the divan and left him to do as he liked, to sit down or to stand. She was depressed and unhappy, but she leaned back against a cushion and said with a shrug, "I think you were crazy to come back to this town if you didn't have to. *Did* you have to?"

Her eyes were wide and deeply blue, and when she looked up at him with such impersonal interest he was almost sorry to have dug such a deep trench between them. He'd spent two weeks digging it. It was what he had wanted and according to specifications, and now it was too wide and deep to hop over. "No, I didn't have to," he said. "I liked it here, last year."

"You'll like it again, I guess. Well. . . ." She smiled at him then, a sad, tremulous smile, and said, "I'm glad you came over, Tim. I'll see you at school tomorrow."

"Are we still friends?" He blurted out the question because he had forgotten how sweet Patty could be. She was so sweet and young; and he was ashamed, a little too late, at having hurt her.

"Of course," she said. "Why not?" She slid her hands beneath her and leaned forward. "My goodness, Tim," she asked, "why shouldn't we be friends?"

"I don't know. I thought you might be sore because I hadn't written to you or called up when I got here. I was a little embarrassed to come over and see you."

"How silly." Her laugh was low and bubbly, with no truant sob caught in. She was playing a part for all she was worth, and it suddenly came to her that she was sitting there like a teacher with a disobedient pupil standing before her. "Lucky you!" she cried, jumping up before he might think so, too. "You don't have to study, but I do."

"Need some help?"

"No, thanks. I only have a chart to make, and I don't mind charts. They always seem so neat and impersonal, and they make me forget that real people did the things I'm printing in."

It was the way she had talked with him last spring, spilling out thoughts that nobody else could inspire, and she laughed her bubbly laugh again. "You'll have to move on now," she said, "so I can put William the Conqueror in his neat little square. Homework has to come before everything else."

She chattered on while she eased him adroitly toward the door, and they stood on the steps batting last year's conversational ball back and forth. But when he had gone and she had flung one last, laughing sally after him, she ran back through the house and flung herself on her bed.

"I hate him," she sobbed, "I hate him, hate him, *hate* him! Oh, what am I going to do?"

She lay there for a long, long time, drenching her pillow with tears, despising Tim and the string of empty years ahead. She heard her mother and father come up from the basement, and despised them, too, for laughing and being so happy in the living room. "Everyone in the whole world is happy but me," she moaned. "Everyone has somebody but *me!* It's all Ginger's fault."

The pain eased a little when she had someone to blame. Ginger had felt so important to be calling up and saying she was bringing Tim over. Ginger wanted Tim. She wanted all the boys. She fed them and kept them hanging around her house. "I wouldn't stoop so low," Patty mumbled, with little blubbery hiccups. "If Tim can't like me for myself and can't see that I'm a thousand times more attractive than Ginger is, he can stay over there forever. I hope he does!"

She dragged herself up on the bed and stared across the lawns at Ginger's dark bedroom window. "Oh, she's gone with him!" she wailed, and flung herself down again.

"Hey, punk." Douglas was coming along the hall. "Have you gone to bed?"

She hadn't heard him come in and it was too late to get up and close her door. She couldn't stop him, so she cut off her sobs and hoped he wouldn't see her. But he snapped on the overhead light.

"Now what's wrong, punk?" he asked, with brotherly clumsiness.

"Go away."

Patty dissolved in tears again, but he turned out the light and felt his way around her bed to sit down on its twin. "Did Phil Lebensdorfer make you sore?"

Patty couldn't answer. He wouldn't understand, not with Bonnie going gabble, gabble, gabble in the living room, and happy days ahead. She could only sob and push his hand away when it patted her shoulder.

"Look, punk," he said, showing that he had come back to her room for a purpose, "Mom said that Tim Ford was here. Did you two have a quarrel?"

"No!" Patty raised herself on her elbows and swung her head back and forth like a caged lion.

"Then what happened? Something did," he told her. "You were as happy as a kitten at dinner. What was it?"

"Ginger," she answered. "Your wonderful Ginger threw

her personality around and got him over there first. She
talked him out of liking me."

"Oh, now, punk, I won't buy that. Tim's no pushover."

"But she *did!*" It was a release to condemn Ginger, so
Patty argued, "She talked him out of being my—the best
friend I have in the world. *She did!*"

"Now, listen, punk." Douglas took her by her elbows
and hauled her up to a sitting position. "I told you last
night that you have to be sincere. Are you crying because
Tim got over the going-steady business, or are you mad at
Ginger?"

"Both," Patty wept. "They fluffed me off, between
them."

"Not Ginger. Tim, maybe, but not Ginger. I wondered
why Tim didn't write to you, if you two were as solid as
you seemed to think you were, but eventually I decided
that the thinking must be more on your side than his. Are
you sure you didn't just *think* you were going steady?"

"No!" Patty shouted at him. "Does Bonnie just think
you are?"

"Bonnie's a lot older than you and she has good sense.
I don't know what to say to you, punk, because you won't
listen. You know as well as I do that Tim's folks don't go
for the steady business, so what do you want the guy to
do? He got the hot treatment at home last year, Mom said
so, and maybe he's had it again. I'll be darned if I'd be so
all-fired sunk because a guy decides he wants to play the
field. And I wouldn't lie there and blame Ginger, either.
I might blame any of the other girls you run around with,
but not Ginger."

"Oh, no? She's gone off with him to see the rest of the
gang."

Patty pointed an accusing finger at the window, but Douglas's eyes didn't follow it. He studied Patty instead. She annoyed him. She was whipping up a storm and being dramatic over something that would probably iron itself out if she gave it time and handled it right, and was being infantile about a status that, so far as he could see, was unchanged. Then he reminded himself that pride is a precious possession. Patty's pride had been hurt. Her silly, feminine pride.

"Look, Patty, honey," he said, "I've been pretty rough on you, too. I really rubbed it in last night, didn't I?"

The blue sapphires in Patty's eyes were dimmed with crystal drops, which was just as well, because no surprise could show through when she stared at him. She had twisted Douglas's criticism into compliments, and only now did she remember that he didn't approve of her; and it dawned on her for the first time that perhaps no one appreciated her. Dismay spread in a slow, hot blush, and she threw herself down on her face again. "Go away," she moaned. "No one understands me."

"Who could?" Douglas got up to go back and report to his parents. "That kid defeats me," he told them, closing the hall door behind him. "She honestly thinks she has good sense."

Patty heard the door close, and got up to slam her own shut. Privacy was what she wanted, she told herself. If people didn't care enough to help her, they might at least leave her alone. And they might keep their laughter down so she didn't have to hear it. She felt her way back to her bed and huddled down again as the distant telephone began to ring.

"Patty, dear," she heard her mother say at her door,

"Ginger wants to talk to you," but she pretended not to hear. "Patty?"

"I've gone to bed," she had to mumble, if she was ever to have quiet again.

"All right, dear, I'll tell her."

She could hear her mother talking in her room across the hall, and her voice went on much longer than it should have to relay a simple message, so Patty had to get up again and open her door a crack. "Oh, Ginger, dear," she heard, "I'm sure Patty doesn't think that. . . . Yes, I understand how it looked, and I'm sure Patty does, too. . . . Yes, of course, I'll tell her, honey. . . . Oh, I'm sure she'll pick you up on her way to school. I'll remind her to, and I'm sure she'll stop for you just as she always does."

"I'll never stop for her again!" Patty stormed, but under her breath, flinging off her clothes. "I don't want Tim back, but I'm going to get him. And then I'm going to laugh, and laugh, and laugh, at you both. *I'll do it.* You just *watch* me do it! Nobody can treat me any old way and get by with it!"

Ginger, replacing her own telephone, had much the same thought. "Patty won't come by," she sighed, "I know she won't. If she wants Tim back, I wish she could get him. I don't think he acted very fair, and I'm glad I told him so. And I'm glad I wouldn't go over to Spark Plug's with him, or wherever he went afterward. I would have, if he'd brought Patty back with him. Oh, dear."

It was after nine o'clock and she still had studying to do. She couldn't concentrate on arithmetic when a personal problem wouldn't add up right, and she asked herself how a day that had started out so glowingly could turn into such a mess.

71

She walked over to her bedroom window that faced Spark Plug's driveway, and stood looking out at Beauty. Beauty wasn't covered with her tarpaulin tonight. The desk light shone on her head lamps that stuck out like a bug's eyes, and on her big, round wheel, and made little shiny streaks along her black leather seat.

"I sat right there this afternoon," Ginger thought, leaning on the sill and pressing her nose against the screen. "And I drove along and had a wonderful time."

The Blakes' back door opened, and she saw Spark Plug come out and go into his garage. She knew what he was going to do, and when he came back with the big folded tarpaulin in his arms, she watched him stop to look up at the stars in a black sky.

"I don't think it's going to rain," she called softly, waiting while he walked over to stand under her window.

"Hi," he said. "It's swell about Tim coming back, isn't it? He has to take some extra tutoring, but he thinks he'll graduate O.K. . . . . Was he over to your house?"

"Yes, and at Patty's," Ginger answered loyally. "I guess he was making the rounds. Did he—did he say anything much to you?"

"Sure. Why not? He said he wants to help work on the car when he has time."

"I mean—oh, never mind."

Ginger realized that Spark Plug wouldn't know what Tim was talking about if he branched away from school and cars, and, furthermore, he wouldn't care. "I guess he'll be a big help to you," she said.

"Sure, I can use him." Spark Plug squinted up at the sky again and decided, "I don't think it'll rain tonight.

You want to help me with the brakes tomorrow? Steve can't make it."

"Oh, I'd love to!" Ginger answered so quickly that she had to stop and hedge. "I mean—will Tim be there?" she asked.

"I don't know. Does it matter?"

It mattered a lot. It mattered that Patty would see her with him.

"Since when did you have to have Tim around?" Spark Plug asked, and she thought she detected the faintest shadow of a scowl on his face. "I thought you just liked to work on the car."

"Oh, I do." Ginger rested her elbows on the sill and cradled her cheeks in her hands. "It's just that I thought you might not need me," she said, wishing she could tell him of the rift between Patty and Tim. "I don't want to bother you."

"You don't bother me. Come on over."

He turned away, but she called softly to him, "Spark Plug, are you going to Mary Lou's birthday party Saturday night?"

"Nope, it's my bowling night. Why? Did you want me to take you?"

"I thought it would be nice if you would. You see. . . ."

Up cropped the problem of Patty and Tim again. Tim was sure to ask her and she needed a valid excuse to refuse. How to explain it without betraying a confidence? "I thought if you asked me," she said, "I wouldn't have to go with someone else. It's a boy I like, but I don't want to go to a party with him."

"Bill Templeton?" he guessed.

"Oh, no."

"Steve? Pete?" Spark Plug considered Tim automatically spoken for, so didn't bother to name him, and for that Ginger was thankful. "Well," he said at her head-shakes, "I'll try to make it. If I can find someone else to bowl in my place on the team, I will. You're pretty good about helping me, so maybe I ought to take you. Mom keeps telling me I ought. See you tomorrow."

He went back to put his tarpaulin in the garage, and Ginger sent her silent thanks to his mother. "You helped me out of a tough spot," she told the light in the Blakes' living-room window. "I was afraid I might have to say I was sick, and stay home."

She sat down at her desk, then pushed her books away and put her head down. Everything seemed so lonely without her best friend.

Chapter 6

Ginger ate her breakfast standing at the counter and watching Patty's back door. She watched as long as she could; and when the clock above the refrigerator told her she would have to start for school or be late, she picked up her books and hurried to the highway. Patty wasn't rounding her own corner and no one was on the hill, so Ginger began to run.

She was breathless when she reached the long cement ramp that led up to her home room, and she tried to shift her books enough to open her purse and take out her comb. The purse should have been left in her locker. Flatly inconspicuous as it was, Mr. Stillman was sure to look accusingly at it, and might even remark in his cold, sarcastic way, that girls who laid money on their desks deserved to lose it.

Ginger had no time to go back, so she rubbed her hot face on her short cotton sleeve while she tugged at the purse's stubborn zipper. Her books started to slide, the purse popped open suddenly, and silver coins and her lipstick spilled out. To be late was worse than to lose her lunch money. The coins rolled down the ramp like little runaway wheels, and there was no one below her to stop them.

75

"Oh, golly," she groaned, just watching them go.

And then Bill Templeton shot through the wide front door. He, too, was running, but he stopped to plant his foot on a quarter and scoop up a dime. "I'll get 'em," he said.

"Oh, thanks." Ginger righted her books and retrieved the lipstick, grateful that his shoes were so big and that he could scoop with such accuracy. And when he poured the coins into her hand, she thanked him again and said with a grin, "You should have kept some out for a tip."

"Maybe I did, you won't know till you count 'em," he answered. "Come on, we've still got time to make it."

He was a senior in Spark Plug's class, and he hustled her along the corridor to her own door. "Be good," he said, as he went on; and then he called back, "I'll come over to Spark Plug's if I get through football practice in time. Are you going to Mary Lou's party?"

"I think so."

Heads in eight long rows turned inquisitively toward the door, and up at the front of the room, Mr. Stillman's chair scraped back. Only one head didn't turn, and that was Patty's. Ginger slid into her seat just as the final gong rang.

"Virginia?" Mr. Stillman said angrily, standing tall and straight. "I assume that you knew the first bell had rung before you came in?"

"No, sir." Ginger stopped restacking her books and rose again on trembling legs. "I was awfully late," she said in apology. "I was trying to hurry, and I—I kept dropping things."

"A very convenient way to make an engagement."

"Oh, it wasn't that way, Mr. Stillman," Ginger tried to

explain. "Bill wasn't asking me for a date. He was only trying to step on my money."

Someone snickered, and Mr. Stillman leaped from his low platform and tramped along the aisle. His wife had been in more pain than usual that morning, the children more demanding, and here was a luckless victim to vent his ill-humor on. Ginger didn't know it until Steve told her later, but when he towered above her, a whole roomful of boys turned sidewise in their seats and were ready to rise to her defense.

"You will remain after school," he said, sensing the hostility when he reached out to confiscate her purse. "Class, come to attention."

Ginger sat down again and bent her head. She had been frightened when Mr. Stillman had come rushing at her, and her hands trembled when she tried to find her theme and the English book she would need for her first class. She couldn't see. And when Steve leaned forward in his seat behind her, and whispered, "Take it easy. Don't let the old goat shake you up," she couldn't answer with so much as a nod. It seemed a long time before her heart stopped racing and she could look across at Patty, who sat with her hands folded, waiting for a bell to call her to class.

Surely, she'll speak to me, *now,* Ginger thought, keeping close to Patty in the crowded hall. I'm still scared about the way Mr. Stillman acted, but it would be worth it if Patty would tell me how sorry she was and—and take some of the blame. She knows why I was late.

But Patty dodged between chattering classmates and caught up with Jane McGuire.

The morning that had begun so badly disintegrated like

a paper towel dropped in water. Ginger's chart, so hurriedly done, was graded a U. She became completely lost in the sub plot of *A Tale of Two Cities,* and was unable to explain intelligently how she had arrived at the price a farmer paid for a cow, after selling fifty hens and his grain, buying three bushels of seed and renting a tractor.

Mr. Stillman still held her lunch ticket, and the money she had brought for dessert and extra milk, so she had to borrow a coupon from Mary Lou. She borrowed a comb and a lipstick, too, then sat at the next table to Patty.

She tried twice to smile at Patty, staring straight at her and willing her to return the smile, but both times Patty turned her head quickly and said something to Jane, beside her. Ginger tried to listen to the talk around her. It swung from Tim's unexpected reappearance to the weird behavior of Mr. Stillman.

"Honestly," Mary Lou said, after Steve had told how the boys were ready to charge like an army if he so much as touched Ginger, "I knew the man was grouchy, but I never thought he could be actually *dangerous.*"

"Maybe he didn't mean to be." Ginger could forgive Mr. Stillman if only Patty would look her way. "He's so big he scares you, but he might not know it."

"Oh, pooh!" Mary Lou tossed her mane of drab hair that was always held back with a clutter of bobby pins, and said positively, "He lives down our block, and he yells at his kids from morning till night. Hey, Tim!" she suddenly called, standing up and waving her paper napkin. "Come over here."

Ginger wanted to sink through the floor. Tim was making his way between the tables, and he stopped at Mary Lou's shout. "Hi," he said to Patty as he passed her; and he pulled out the empty chair beside Ginger and sat down. "What gives?" he asked, looking across her. "I'm through here until Monday, so spill it fast."

"My party," Mary Lou answered pertly, reaching for what was left of Steve's apple cobbler. "I've got a new dress for it and I'll be the prettiest girl there."

"Come again? With your waistline?"

He winked at Ginger, but she had pushed back her chair. "I have to go," she said. "I have some work to make up."

She got up and started out, then, with sudden resolve, walked straight to Patty's table and stopped beside her. "Plus," she said unhappily, "I want to talk to you about—about what happened last night. Will you walk down the hall with me?"

"I haven't finished my lunch."

"Shall I wait for you?"

"Don't bother. Jane and I are going down to the corner for a candy bar."

"If Fred's still hung up with the coach, I am," Jane said with a rueful laugh. "Football is ruining my love life." And not being in the same home room with Ginger and Patty, she asked, "What's all this I hear about you and old Stillman mixing it up this morning? Did he really shake you?"

"Of course he didn't." Even with Patty eating cream pie as if she wanted to make it last forever, Ginger had to smile. "He just got cross because I was late," she said.

"That's not the way I heard it. Biff Dunnington told me that all the boys in the room rushed at him. He said. . . ."

"Don't believe him." Ginger listened to Patty murmur

that she was going back to buy another bottle of milk, and turned away. It was no use waiting. Patty wouldn't come back. "Nothing like that happened at all," she said. "He just yelled a little, that's all. I'll see you in class."

Mr. Stillman was sitting at his desk when Ginger tiptoed into the room. She didn't want to be alone with him and would have slipped out again but there was no place else to go. She had decided to write Patty a note, so she took out her pen and a sheet of paper as quietly as she could. He didn't seem to know she was there.

Miles Stillman was having as much trouble with a column of figures as Ginger had had with the problem of the farmer who had bought a cow. His wife needed an operation, and no matter how many times he added up its cost, they couldn't afford it. Not even with the five hundred dollars he would ask the bank to lend him. Not on his small salary. Not with hiring someone to care for the children and with the long recovery period his wife would have to have afterward. Every now and then he took a bite from a ragged-looking sandwich while he scratched out some figures and substituted others; and it wasn't until he spilled coffee from his thermos bottle and reached out for a blotter that he looked up and saw Ginger.

His first reaction was anger. He had let his temper lash out that morning, and now its target had come back to spy on him! She wanted to watch him eat his slapped-together, homemade lunch so she could giggle about it to her friends. But even though he stared at her, she didn't look up. She was writing something, and every now and then she wiped her eyes with the back of her hand.

"Virginia?" he said, sounding stern without consciously intending to.

"Yes, Mr. Stillman?"

She raised her head and sat with her pen poised above a half-written word. They were in private worlds of misery, and they looked blankly at each other until he broke the silence. "I thought you were to stay *after* school, not during the lunch hour."

"I was. But you see—well, I can leave if you want me to."

"Come to my desk."

Ginger got up slowly and walked to the edge of his platform. She saw his scowl, the dark lock of hair that hung over his forehead, even a tiny crumb of bread on his chin. She was a little afraid but she tried not to show it.

"Tell me, Virginia," he said, wiping off the crumb, "do you think it was right for you to make all that racket this. morning?"

"No, sir."

"Then why did you do it?"

"Well, you see, I was late." Ginger had never been able to explain anything unless she began at the beginning, so she said, "I was late leaving home, and I ran so fast that I didn't have time to stop at my locker, and my hair looked so awful that I was trying to open my purse—to get my comb out, you know—and all my money flew out."

She had to pause for a breath, so he asked, "And then?"

"Bill Templeton came along. He was almost late, too, but he stopped to pick it all up—the money, I mean—and we didn't know we were practically shouting. I'm awfully sorry."

"I'm sorry, too."

Ginger believed that any person who did wrong, knowingly or otherwise, should be prompt to apologize. And since she was doing the best she could, with both Patty and him, she took it for granted that he referred to his own behavior. "Oh, that's all right," she said, to his great dismay. "I don't blame you for being cross about it. I deserved it. But you did scare me."

"I did? How?" Mr. Stillman was surprised at himself for having let his misinterpreted sentence slide by and for inviting a further opinion on his behavior, but what was done was done, so he crossed his arms on his desk and waited for her to go on. He had an appointment at the bank at three-thirty, so it was just as well to get this disciplinary conference over.

"Well," Ginger said thoughtfully, "Miss Maxwell was our home room teacher last year, and she was always so pleas . . . that is, we've never had a man before—not even in junior high. We did in grammar school," she corrected herself, "because the principal taught the sixth grade."

"And you think a man home-room teacher is different from a woman?"

"I suppose so." Ginger blinked at him while she thought that over. "My father is different from my mother," she said, when she had made up her mind. "Mom is sort of easy on me, but when Daddy lays down the law, he means it."

"And I'm like your father."

"No." Ginger couldn't let him believe that. Mr. Stillman was a poor comparison to her father, and she looked down at his desk while she considered an appropriate answer.

A yellow scratch pad lay there. It was covered with figures. Figures were scribbled in all directions. Some had circles and stars drawn around them, and others were followed by such words as "hospital" and "daily expenses." There were even problems in multiplication and short division, and doodling all over the page. "I expect everybody has to be different, and have different ways of doing things," she said slowly. Then she lifted her eyes. "We're a pretty good class when you get to know us," she said. "We want you to like us."

Students had begun drifting in, and Mr. Stillman didn't want to be caught eating his lunch. He hastily crumpled up the wax paper that had held his sandwich and reassembled the thermos bottle. "Do you think you can keep out of trouble?" he asked, dropping the thermos bottle into a drawer and the paper into his wastebasket.

"Oh, I hope so."

Three boys were standing in a group, all scowling belligerently, so Ginger flashed Mr. Stillman a smile. "Thanks, loads, for letting me have this chance to explain," she said. And he found himself passing over her small, red purse.

"You'd better put this in your locker, Virginia," he told her. "And you needn't stay after school."

"Oh, thank you." Ginger took the purse, then leaned over his desk again. "Mr. Stillman," she whispered hopefully, "do you think you could do something for me?"

His lecture had turned out to be no lecture at all, and now she was requesting a favor! "What?" he asked with resignation.

"Nobody ever calls me anything but Ginger," she went on, still whispering sociably. "I know it says Virginia on my credits card, but sometimes I forget to answer when you call on me in Latin. You see," she explained, "there were three Virginias when I started in the first grade, so I had to be called. . . ."

"Ginger. I'll remember."

"Oh, thank you again." Ginger backed away as one would from an audience with the king, but she smiled so broadly that the clamps on her braces showed. "Thanks," she repeated, backing all the way into the hall, where she collided with Miss Maxwell.

"Wait. Hold it," Miss Maxwell said with a laugh. "Where do you think you're going?"

"To put my purse in my locker," Ginger answered. "I hope I have time."

Shirley Maxwell was the ideal teacher. She was understanding, strict but never harsh; and if Section B of the tenth grade was, as Ginger had told Mr. Stillman, "a pretty good class," she had made it that way. "I'll keep the purse for you," she offered. "You're coming to club meeting after school, aren't you?"

"I don't think so." For a little while Ginger had forgotten Patty's quarrel with her. Patty didn't belong to the Girls Who Don't Go Steady. She hadn't been asked to join when Mary Lou had formed the club, because she had been going steady with Steve Harding, and later, when she was eligible to be a member, she had huffily said it was silly. "I'm not sure I can come," Ginger said, hoping that Patty might forgive her after school.

"I'll keep your purse, anyway." Miss Maxwell smiled and held out her hand, and Ginger gratefully put the cause of so much trouble into it.

"Miss Maxwell," she asked, "do you like Mr. Stillman?"

"I don't know him very well, dear," Miss Maxwell answered. "This is his first year here, and he seems like a nice young man. He's having a lot of trouble, you know."

"What with?"

Ginger remembered the sheet of yellow paper, so she wasn't surprised to hear, "His wife is quite ill, and he's had to give up the night classes he was taking at Penn to get his Master's. I don't see how the poor man manages, with all the nursing and housework he has to do. Do *you* like him?"

Miss Maxwell, as sponsor for the G.W.D.G.S. girls and a popular chaperone for their parties, had been promptly informed of Ginger's brush with Mr. Stillman. The story grew each time she heard it, so she waited eagerly for Ginger's answer.

"I do, now," Ginger said emphatically. "He's very forgiving and nice."

The warning bell sounded, and determined to be in her seat and ready, Ginger hustled back through the door she had just left. It was the front entrance to the room, and she flashed Mr. Stillman a companionable smile as she went by his desk. She flashed Patty one, too, but both smiles went unanswered. Mr. Stillman was making notes for his Latin class, and Patty was carefully looking the other way.

Ginger sat down to reread what she had written in her note and to finish it if possible; and when Steve leaned over to ask, "What suddenly gives with you and the prof?" she only said, "Don't bother me, now," and continued to read and write at the same time.

Look Plus, the note began. *If we aren't ever going to be friends again, say so. If we are, don't let's waste time being mad. I'm sorry that Tim hurt your feelings and I tried to stop it. I truly did. I don't blame you for being burned—but please, don't be burned at me. I want to be your best friend a. . . .* She finished the *again* and signed the note *Perse.* And she added, *P.S. Sometimes I'm pretty unhappy, too.*

That ought to tell her, she thought, folding the paper. Then she began to wonder how she could make Patty accept the note, and finally turned around to Steve. "How about you giving this to Patty for me?" she asked. "She won't speak to me."

"You're a dope." Steve took the wad of paper and leaned forward to say, "I know all about it—Tim told me. You're being the cue ball. Do you want to go to Mary Lou's party with me?"

Invitations were pouring in too fast. Ginger shook her head because Spark Plug had courageously offered himself as a sandbag against the flood, but she said over her shoulder, "Ask Patty."

"The answer is, no, again. I'll give the note to your chum, but that ends it. Here we go."

A bell shrilled, Latin students remained and the others shuffled out to start the last half of a long, hot day.

The Latin hour was endless and tiresome. Ginger was pleased to have Mr. Stillman look at her as if he knew which one she was when he called on her to recite, and to use her nickname, but she had to fight off sleep during a study period afterward. No breeze came through the open windows, and she felt sticky and hot. But at last it was over. Friday, her most bearable day of the whole school week had come to an end.

Ginger retrieved her purse from Miss Maxwell, but

didn't wait for the other club members to gather. There had been no answer to her note, not even a flicker of a nod from Patty, so she trudged home and sat lonesomely at the kitchen table, drinking a glass of milk.

Spark Plug had two helpers in his back yard today, Steve —and Tim, and she sat watching them pull on their stained white coveralls. She even looked listlessly at the box of chocolate cookies her mother had left out on the counter for her.

She had sat there for almost half an hour when Tim opened the screen door and came in.

"Oh, go away!" she cried. "You've caused me enough trouble."

"Spark Plug sent me," he answered, not moving. "He wants you to come out and drive again."

Spark Plug had seen Ginger outlined in the big window, and with his customary shyness had sent one of his henchmen on an errand of mercy. Steve had been told to go, but because he was squirting oil on a rusty bolt that was beginning to give, Tim had offered to.

"I don't dare come over while you're there," Ginger explained unhappily. "Don't you know I'm trying to make up with Patty?"

"Aw, come on." He leaned against the counter while he studied her, and finally said, "If it will patch things up for you, I'll go over to her house and drag her back."

"You couldn't." Ginger knew Patty even better than her parents did, so she said, "She hates us both, by now. You can have the cookies Mom bought, but I'll have to stay here. Go on, take them."

To forego driving Beauty was her greatest sacrifice to devotion, and she watched Tim pick up the box. "You're being a stupe," he said, tapping it against his hand. "Do you think Patty's worrying about how you feel?"

"That isn't the point. I only know that she thinks you and I, both, are traitors, and is hurting inside as much as I am. It doesn't matter what hurts you, Tim," she said. "Whatever it is—it hurts."

"Okay. If that's the way you want it." Tim opened the door again and banged it shut behind him.

She watched him cross the lawn and show the box to Spark Plug. Spark Plug had been standing on the grass, assembling a motor part, and his hands stopped moving. He looked serious. He talked earnestly for a few minutes, then laid the part on Beauty's running board and wiped his hands on the seat of his coveralls before he walked over to Ginger's window.

"You can come out now, chum," he said, looking up at her. "Tim's leaving."

"Oh, I don't want him to do that!" Ginger leaned close to the screen and pleaded, "Tell him to stay."

"Not a chance." His square face was set and his frank gray eyes looked unyieldingly up at her. "Beauty's my car," he said. "If the Joes want to come and help me work on her I'm glad to have 'em. But there's not going to be any unpleasantness in my back yard. Any square who causes trouble will have to stay away."

Ginger's lips opened, but he went on, "If Tim and Patty have had a bust-up they'll have to settle it between them and not put you in the middle. I told him that, and he's not sore about it. Come on out."

He turned away, and Ginger had never admired him so much. Spark Plug, her unexpected defender! Driving Beauty wouldn't be half the fun it had been yesterday, but Spark Plug wanted her to do it. Sane, wonderful Spark Plug.

"I'll be there in a minute," she called, reaching across the table for her flat red purse and taking out her comb and lipstick.

Chapter 7

Saturday, warm, sunny, and long awaited by many, was a trying day for some because of one girl's tangled affairs. Spark Plug, who didn't want to go to Mary Lou's party, anyway, had to leave his fascinating car to have his hair cut and to hunt all over town for a substitute for his bowling team. Ginger stayed indoors all day, waiting for the telephone to ring, and watching Patty's back door. Her mother and father were discouraged with her. They alternated between pity and a desire to shake some sense into her, and wished she would either go to the movies or someplace with the girls. Patty's house was in a state of unhappy confusion, with Douglas leaving for college on the one o'clock train.

"For goodness' sake, Patty, stop moping," Mrs. Palmer scolded, pausing in Patty's doorway and frowning at the prone figure on the bed. "The world hasn't come to an end."

"I'm not moping." Patty sat up and tossed aside the magazine she had been pretending to read.

"Then get up and help me. You know I'm trying to pack Douglas's clothes, and you can at least get his white shirts out of the laundry package or make lunch, or something. I don't see why you want to lie there just because one certain boy isn't taking you to a party."

"I'm not going to the party."

"Oh, nonsense." Mrs. Palmer had no time either to coax her daughter into a better humor or to argue with her, but she did wait long enough to say, "I wouldn't let Tim or any other boy know he could make me miserable. I'd be the prettiest girl at the party and have the best time." And at that, Patty flopped down again.

"Go away," she moaned. "Oh, please, *please* let me alone!"

There was nothing to do but to leave, since Douglas needed her more today, but Jane Palmer went back to the living room where her husband was putting new laces in Douglas's ski boots. "Ben," she suggested, stopping beside him, "why don't we drive Doug up to Providence instead of sending him on the train?"

"What did you say?"

He looked up with a leather thong poised above an eyelet, and she hurried on, "It's such a beautiful day. We could start right after lunch, spend the night in that quaint little inn we found last spring, and deliver Douglas early tomorrow morning. Then we could show Patty the town and the college. We'd be back home on Monday."

"Now whatever put such an idea as that into your head?" he asked. "You're having three couples here to supper tomorrow night."

"But I could postpone it. They wouldn't care." Just then, Douglas came through the dining room, the package of laundry in his arms, and she turned to him brightly. "How would you like it," she asked, "if we make a heyday of your departure and all drive you up to Brown?"

"I wouldn't." He set the bundle in a chair and ripped open its brown wrapping paper. "I'm going to college. I'm going to get off the train like the rest of the fellows."

"But, darling," she protested, "it's such beautiful weather and we'd all love the drive. We'd let you out at your dorm and you wouldn't see us again."

"No, thanks." Douglas laid a shirt of his father's aside and went on with his sorting. "It was a nice try, Mom," he said, "but it didn't work. I'm sorry for Patty, but I'm disgusted with her, too—and carting her off for a week end won't help her grow up. I've got dates with three fraternities tomorrow and I don't intend to walk into their clubs holding my little sister by the hand. I don't intend to show her the sacred portals of Brown, either."

"But, darling, I promise. . . ."

"No, Mom." Douglas picked up the shirts he had chosen and shook his head. "You're being as dumb as Patty," he said. "Isn't she, Dad?"

"I'd say so." Ben Palmer passed over the laced boots and added slyly, "Except that she's grabbing at a chance to see how her little boy is bedded down and to meet his roommate."

"I'll bring him home some week end. Thanks for fixing my boots, Dad."

Douglas gave his mother's shoulder an understanding pat and went on to the hall. He saw Patty scurry back into her room, and, knowing that she had been hopefully eavesdropping, stopped to look in at her. She was standing before her mirror, and he said gruffly, "Remember what I told you the other night, punk? You can't expect other people to carry you around on a satin pillow."

"I—I d-don't."

She wiped away a tear and tried to run a comb through her curls, so blindly and with such a trembling hand, that he said more kindly, "I know it's hard, punk, but these things happen."

"If I could—could just go away for a few days," she sobbed, "I could—manage before the next party."

"You could manage now, if you'd only try," he answered, unmoved in his decision to get off a train and share a taxi with other students. "Most of your crowd goes in a gang. Girls go to parties together and boys don't have dates. They pick 'em up when they get there."

"You don't *know.*"

Patty's tears flowed faster and she made a real effort to check them. She combed and wiped her eyes on the back of her hand until Douglas, truly anxious to help, suggested tactlessly, "Why don't you and Ginger go together? She doesn't care if she hasn't a date."

"She hates me! She's the one," Patty turned around to declare hotly, "who took Tim away from me in the first place. She'll go to the party with him, you wait and see."

"No, she won't. You've got her all wrong." Douglas had talked with his parents about Ginger's agonized telephone call, and even though time was rushing along, he took another minute or two to explain, "Ginger's loyal, Patty, you know she is. No matter how mad you are at Tim, you oughtn't take it out on her. Why don't you call her up and let her work out something with you? Go on, do it."

"No." Patty dropped the comb and pushed past him. "I'm not going to the party, and that's final," she said. "I don't care what everybody thinks of me or if Ginger gloats and Tim laughs."

"Okay." He followed her out and returned to his packing. His own new life was beginning. And while he locked the brass clasps on a mammoth old wardrobe trunk and closed a new leather suitcase, he could hear voices in the living room. Patty was loudly calling her best friend a female Brutus and repeating her intentions to stay home. To Douglas, from a distance, it seemed that his parents sharply contradicted the first and calmly accepted the latter.

The matter wasn't mentioned again, because trains run on schedule and cause hurry and flurry, no matter how well organized a departure may be. The trunk had to be loaded into a friend's station wagon, a forgotten raincoat stuffed into the suitcase, Douglas's wallet checked to make sure his ticket was in it, and a drooping Patty told good-by and left to do the dishes. But just before he climbed aboard the sleek local which would take him as far as New York, Douglas said to both parents, "Now, stop worrying about Patty. The punk's going to snap out of it—she always does. You're too soft, though. Keep her in line, this time, and make her behave."

"I wish we knew how," Jane Palmer sighed to her husband, waving valiantly as long as she could see Douglas's window. "And I wish Doug hadn't grown up so fast and left us forever. It's never going to be the same again. From now on, we'll only have him for vacations—and then he'll get married and go off somewhere else to live."

"Philadelphia has good newspapers, if that's what he chooses," Ben Palmer answered, feeling a tightness behind his eyes which he attributed to staring so hard after the train. "We haven't lost Doug."

"And then he'll get married," she went on, reluctant to be consoled, "either to Bonnie or some other nice girl.

Oh, well," she said, hooking her arm through his as they walked along the suburban platform to their car, "my mother thinks she's lucky if she sees us and the children twice a year. What shall we do about the one we have left at home?"

"Patty?" He laughed ruefully, then added with resignation, "Why, we'll cancel our plans for the party at the club tonight and stay home and baby sit. If she won't go, she won't go, that's all."

"I'll call Mary Paxton as soon as I get home and tell her we can't come. Oh, dear."

Jane Palmer wasn't thinking of her own lost evening, she was sighing over her child's disappointment. Douglas was rolling along on his train, happily expectant, and Patty was at home with the weeps. "Darn it!" she said.

They let themselves in to silence. They put away the skis that Douglas had refused to carry with him, looking, he said, "like a tourist." They straightened the living room, and then Mrs. Palmer went back to have a secret cry in the room which still held the warmth and presence of her son.

"Mother?" Patty called. "That dumb Steve telephoned and said he'd take me to the party."

"Oh, good." Jane Palmer's spirits lifted, and she went on to Patty's door.

"But I told him I wouldn't go."

Patty was lying on the bed again. She had her almost hairless Teddy bear beside her, and her manicure kit. Teddy was always a handkerchief for Patty's tears and the manicure kit hadn't been opened.

"It's up to you," her mother answered, remembering Douglas's last instructions and trying to live up to them by not coaxing Patty. "If you want to miss the fun, that's your business."

She stoically set Douglas's room to rights, careful to leave as much of his personality in it as she could, but making it neat. Then she baked two tins of his favorite cookies. Somewhere in the back of her mind was the idea of mailing a box of them to him. But no doubt, she thought wryly, dumping the cookies into a jar, dozens of other mothers were thinking the same thing. And at last it was five-thirty, and time to start dinner.

The telephone rang when she was peeling potatoes at the sink, and by the time she had reached across the breakfast-room table and picked up the receiver Patty was on the extension, so she put it down again.

"Oh, *Mother!*" Patty screeched, standing in the door to the dining room, her hands clasped under her chin, her face abloom with smiles. "That was Tim! He *wants* to take me."

"He does?" Mrs. Palmer laid down her knife and turned around. She could see her husband beyond Patty, standing in the living room archway, shaking his head. "Do you mean to the party?" she asked.

"Oh, *yes!*" Patty's blissful sigh said that there was no other place in the world to go, and she explained, "He's sorry that I got such a wrong impression about him, and he would have asked me sooner but he wasn't at school this afternoon, and then he had to go clear out to the country on an errand for his grandmother. He'd thought he'd be at Spark Plug's, but he had to leave. Then he went to the country."

"Oh." Mrs. Palmer had no way of knowing that Tim had driven out to the country in a disturbed state of mind, but she sensed it. "You aren't going to the party, dear," she said. "Don't you remember? You told us so."

"But that was before *Tim* asked me!" Patty cried.

"But not before Steve did. You said you weren't going, so Daddy and I canceled our plans. I'm afraid you'll have to stay home, dear."

"Oh, *Mother!*" Patty flung herself across the kitchen and onto a chair. *"I can't bear it!"* she cried, crossing her arms on the table and hiding her face in them.

"Patty!" Her father's unexpected voice brought her head up and she stared tearfully at him while he said, "Staying home from the party was your decision, not ours. You've repeated it all day. You've been disagreeable and annoying. Let's hear no more about it."

"But, Daddy, I'm sorry. I didn't mean to be cross, but . . . I'm sorry."

She wanted to rise and go to him, but his stern expression was too forbidding. He didn't look as if he would want her coaxing arms around his neck, as he was saying, "You've pouted and wept for two days and spoiled our last hours with Douglas. You've even lost your best friend. If I were Ginger I'd never forgive you."

"I'll call her up," Patty said quickly, interrupting the list of her misdemeanors and reaching for the telephone. "I'll tell her I'm sorry, too. She—and whoever she's going to the party with—can double date with us. Ginger won't care if I misunderstood about things and got mad. She. . . ."

"You may call her tomorrow if you like, but not tonight. If you feel genuinely sorry, you may call her tomorrow."

"But, Daddy. . . ."

He had told her everything that he had come in to say, but he paused in the doorway for one last warning. "You are not going to the party tonight, Patricia," he said. "What you do about a valuable friendship is up to you—tomorrow. You can try to salvage it or you can throw it away. But remember this—at your age, boys will come and boys will go, but a true friendship with someone of your own sex will last a lifetime."

He went back to his evening newspaper, and Patty looked pleadingly to her mother, but she was turning down the flame under the potatoes. "He's mean," Patty grumbled to herself, so low that she thought no one could hear it. "He's just—plain—mean."

But her mother heard. Patty's lips were moving, and between looking and listening, she had read them. "What was that you said?" she asked.

"I. . . ." Patty was caught, so she hung her head and finished reluctantly, "I said that Daddy's mean. I'm sorry I said it."

"I should think you would be. You're the one who is being mean. Mean to us and to others who love you. I know this punishment seems hard to you," she said carefully, "but pride should mean more. You should have valued Ginger and Steve, instead of grasping at a last-minute date with a boy who only made it because his conscience hurt him. That's what Tim did, Patty, so face it."

"I can't." Patty looked up, her blue eyes misty. "Boys have always liked me," she said plaintively.

"I know, dear, but. . . ." The chops needed turning, so Jane Palmer opened the wall broiler and turned them before she went on, ". . . you can't push things. You're too young to go steady. Tim sees it and you don't, that's all. He hoped you would fall in line and show good sense. Can't you understand that, dear?"

"I guess so." Patty looked wistfully at the telephone, and asked, "Can I call up Ginger now?"

"Your father said tomorrow."

"I know." Patty looked down at her clasped hands, lost in thought. She was resigned, now, to staying home from the party, but it seemed suddenly wrong to make Ginger suffer. Ginger was her friend, and she shouldn't suffer unhappiness over a crime she hadn't committed. Ginger was loyal and true. Ginger was the dearest girl in the world. "I'll feel awful," Patty murmured, "if I don't tell her I'm sorry for the way I acted."

"Tomorrow," her mother answered, taking down a platter from the overhead cupboard. "You can call Tim, now, and Mary Lou, then help me."

"But what shall I tell Tim?" Patty asked, looking at a telephone that had suddenly become a fearsome thing.

"The truth. That you're restricted. 'Confined to quarters,' as Daddy used to say in the army. You can tell him why or not, just as you choose."

"Why is why?" Patty asked again.

"Because—oh, heavens, you surely must know!" Jane Palmer stopped with one chop hanging from a fork to look at this child of hers who knew only what she wanted to know. "Because you've been grouchy," she said. "You can let it go at that, or you can say that you've been about as stupid and unbearable as a girl can be. Take your choice."

She laid the chop down with the others and went in to set the platter on the dining-room table, straightening the silver that Patty had plopped down any old way. There were only three plates stacked at the head of the table, and Douglas's chair was against the wall instead of where it always had been at mealtime. She ran a loving hand over its back, missing her tall, fine son, then stood listening to Patty trying to explain to someone in a small halting voice:

"I just can't go, Tim, that's all. Doug went away today and Mother and Dad are terribly sunk. I wouldn't feel right to go out and leave them tonight . . . no, I mean it. I'll see you around."

"Well, that's one way out that I hadn't thought of," Mrs. Palmer told herself grimly. Then she suddenly smiled and went in to kiss the top of her husband's head. "Us gals must keep our pride," she said, before she told him what excuse Patty had made.

"Do you think anything we said sank in?"

"I don't know."

She watched Patty carry in the tureens of vegetables, straighten the flat silver that already had been straightened, and whispered, "Praise be to our son, Douglas! His advice was good, and she's being a very meek little girl. Let's hope it lasts."

Chapter 8

"Did you have a good time at the party last night?" Mrs. Johnston asked, watching Ginger ladle a blob of scrambled eggs onto a plate and take a piece of toast from the toaster.

"Umhm. It was nice." Ginger took her breakfast to the table and went back to the refrigerator for the glass of milk on a shelf. "Mary Lou got lots of presents," she said, sitting down. Then she looked listlessly out at the bright Sunday sunshine. "Patty didn't come," she said. "Do you suppose she's sick?"

"What excuse did she give Mary Lou?"

"She said that her mother and father were lonesome because Doug'd left and that they needed her. But of course it wasn't true. Patty never stayed home with them before, and she wouldn't notice if they were lonesome, or not. They wouldn't want her to."

Beauty was standing, high and upright, under her tarpaulin, and Ginger stared at the brown mound she made without knowing it and without listening for whatever answer her mother might make. She was thinking about last night's party.

Spark Plug had good-naturedly hauled her off in his father's sedan, and they had picked up Steve and another couple along the way. Steve had been the first to say that he had offered himself as a human sacrifice to Patty. Then Tim had said it.

Mary Lou's big basement recreation room had been full of music and merriment when Tim had planted himself before her. "Come on, Ginger-cookie," he'd said, just as if he hadn't smashed up Patty's happiness, and hers. "Let's dance."

"I don't feel much like dancing with you," she remembered answering. And at that he had grabbed her and swung her out on the shiny tiled floor. But he hadn't danced. He had simply marked time and let other couples bump and shove him, while he said:

"I telephoned Patty and asked to bring her tonight. I didn't want to, but I did it, because Spark Plug made me feel like a heel. At first she said she'd come, then she called back and said she wouldn't. I think I'm right about easing things off, but I don't want Spark Plug sore at me—or you, either. You know, Ginger-cookie, I've come back to live in this town, and I have to get along in it. If staying solid with Patty is the only way I can do it, I'll have to stay solid. I understand my folks' reasoning, and I don't want to do it, but if I have to I will. I played it all wrong from the first."

It was a long speech, and Ginger listened with her big eyes upturned to his. She understood him, but loyalty to Patty kept her from saying so. "Patty doesn't want you that way," she ventured. "In fact, she doesn't want you at all. I don't think she wants to go steady with you any more than you want to go steady with her."

"Did she say so?"

"No, but she didn't come tonight, did she? Patty has ideals." Ginger hoped the good Lord would forgive her, but she went on, "She's not as feather-brained as she looks, and she's glad to get out of a sticky situation. I *know* she is. Her folks beat on her as much as yours do."

"Then why didn't she come with Steve?" he asked, still unconvinced. "He says he took the dive, too."

"Because she was honest about wanting to stay home with her folks. "Why can't you understand," Ginger pleaded earnestly, "that sometimes a girl would rather stay home and make her parents happy than go out and have fun herself?"

"Ginger-cookie, you're lying." Tim danced her out into the crowd, then, but he looked down at her and winked. "You're just about the best little Ginger-cookie ever made," he said. "Five years from now—if I haven't fallen in love with someone else, and if you're still around—I'm going to ask you to go on a honeymoon with me. Is it a deal?"

"Oh, sure."

Last night, five years had seemed a life span away; but now, sitting at the table over her untouched breakfast, Ginger wished that at least one of those years would pass quickly and move Patty beyond this unhappy time.

"What did you say?" she asked, conscious that her mother was talking to her.

"I asked if Mary Lou liked the flowered scarf you gave her."

"I guess so. She got four more almost like it."

She returned to her musing, but her mother prodded, "What did you do all evening?"

"Oh, we danced," Ginger answered, dragging her thoughts back. "And we played a game where you choose couples and hunt for things—little things, like a postage stamp and a hairpin and a thimble. Everything's right in plain sight, but they're the dickens to see. The prize was two real leather brief cases and I sure wanted to win one— but Spark Plug wasn't much help. I found six things, but he only found two."

She went back to remembering the way Spark Plug had fallen behind. "Listen, pal," he had said, when they were given a pencil and a list of twelve small items to discover, "the way to win this match is to watch where the others go and to study the expressions on their faces. If they find something and write it down, hustle over to the same spot and take a look."

The idea had been sound. She had found a bobby pin in a picture frame that way, and a dollar bill crumpled between the leaves of a plant; but Spark Plug had forgotten his mission. Franny Ager had broken her string of beads, and he had gone crawling around, picking up pearls. "Well, gee," he explained, when Ginger scolded him, "the poor kid was scared stiff. She said they belonged to her mother and had cost fifty bucks. What did you want me to do?"

"Just what you did." He wouldn't have been Spark Plug had he ignored a distress signal; but it did seem ironic, she reflected, that Franny's partner had kept on going and had won the brief cases for them.

That part of the evening had been fun, as had been making ice-cream sodas at a real soda fountain, and watching cubes of ice tumble from a machine into a glass. But all the time and deep inside her heart, Ginger had felt the nagging little worry about Patty.

"Patty had bought a new dress to wear," she looked up

at her mother to say. "I don't think she'd have offered to stay home when she had a new dress, do you?"

"Child, I don't know, so eat your breakfast."

"I think she's sick." Ginger shoved the eggs about, then looked up again. "I really think she's sick," she said, "and I ought to call her up again."

"Don't touch that telephone!"

Katherine Johnston's patience snapped. Ginger had had a new dress for the party, too, yet had gone off in it as if it were an old potato bag. No pirouettes before her mirror, no admiration of her shiny, white teeth. "There must be something simple about a child," she silently told herself, "who has more conscience than common sense." Patty had always lorded it over Ginger, from the time they were small. "You eat your pie first," Mrs. Johnston had overheard Patty say one day, "then if it's good, I'll eat mine." And, obediently, Ginger had chewed up a mouthful of mud.

"You are not talking to Patty until she calls you," she said aloud, also remembering the time, just last winter, when Patty had insisted to all the girls that the correct costume for Ginger's party would be a sweater and skirt, then had shown up herself in a blue velvet dress with a frilly white collar. "You've tried to make up with her, and now your father and I have heard all we want to hear about it. Would you like to go out to the club with us after church, and swim?"

"No. I'm going to Spark Plug's—if Tim isn't there, that is."

"Oh, mercy!" Mrs. Johnston looked out at the Palmers' back door and wished she could have a heart to heart talk with Patty's mother. She knew Jane Palmer in a neighborly way, they had a few mutual friends and met at large parties, but they had never been close. Jane's a sensible girl, she thought, and I don't believe she's any more keen on this silly quarreling than I am. Or Ben either. I wonder if I couldn't ask them over for bridge. And then she sighed. "Parent, keep out," she told herself sternly, knowing that Ginger wouldn't hear her.

Ginger was thinking of something else that Tim had said last night. He had found her sitting on the stairway, stroking Mary Lou's shaggy old dog, and had sat down beside her to ask, "How about going out to your Aunt Margaret's tomorrow? I went out there to pick up Gram today, and Miss Partridge has the cutest batch of puppies you ever saw. French poodles. Have you seen them?"

"Not since they've had their eyes open." Ginger had cuddled the tiny black balls of fluff, and had secretly coveted the fattest, wobbliest one. "I'd love to go," she had said. "That is—well, maybe next week."

Now she asked her mother, "Do you like puppies?"

"Why, I think so, dear." Mrs. Johnston was glad to lay aside a problem that was like a troublesome piece of mending and wouldn't pucker into place, so she answered, "We had old Blossom until you were ten."

"But I mean little puppies," Ginger specified, "the kind that make puddles when you're trying to housebreak them, and are a nuisance."

"Blossom was a puppy when we got her," Mrs. Johnston said with a laugh. "She was a wedding present that chewed up a lot of my other wedding presents. Why?"

"I sort of wish I had one," Ginger said, sighing. "A puppy fills up an awful lot of time, taking care of it and playing with it, I mean." Ginger saw so many lonesome

days ahead that she explained, "Tim was talking about
Aunt Mag's puppies last night. He wants me to go out
and see them."

"Do you want one?"

"I don't know. Aunt Mag told me that she wouldn't
think of selling them, so she's going to give them away to
her very special friends. I expect she's promised all five
of them, by now."

"Shall I ask her?" An only child always needs a pet of
some kind to take the place of a brother or sister; and
with Patty's future companionship in a very doubtful
state, Mrs. Johnston suggested eagerly, "Why don't I yank
your father off of the golf course and have him drive us
out there?"

"We'd better wait and think about it."

Ginger was never one to wait, so her mother looked at
her in perplexity. "Here I am," she went on talking to
herself, as she had for the last half-hour, "willing to give
up my Sunday; willing to puppy-sit and have my rugs
ruined, and she sits there saying that we'd better wait."
Then she said aloud, "Honestly, Ginger, I wish you were
small enough to spank."

And that made Ginger smile. "Here," she said, holding
out her hand, palm up, "you can whack me with your shoe
if you want to. I deserve it."

"But you don't, that's just the trouble. I wish you did.
I wish you would be a little harder to get along with. Not
at home," she amended, "just with your friends. Now,
either eat your breakfast or go clean up your room."

Ginger chose her room, and while she changed the
sheets on her bed, she listened for the telephone to ring
in her mother's room. It kept a dignified silence, quite in

keeping with a Sunday morning, and Ginger had gone to church and come home again before its bell cut loose. And then it only summoned her father.

Patty, so near she could have shouted out of her bedroom window and made Ginger hear, had built her day around the telephone, too. She wanted to use it, but she couldn't. She even sat in the breakfast ell beside it. And at last, just when she had taken a deep breath and was about to reach out and grasp it, she caught a glimpse of Ginger. Ginger was coming down her back steps, headed for Spark Plug's.

"If that's all she cares," Patty cried angrily, "I won't tell her I'm sorry. She knows I am, but if she can't wait even a little while for me to say so, I won't tell her."

It was two o'clock, and Ginger's mother had sent her across the lawn with a bowl of fried chicken for the Blakes' and Johnstons' communal supper.

"Carrying Spark Plug fudge!" Patty scoffed. "That's all she cares about. Just Spark Plug. Everybody could treat me like dirt and I could die, and she wouldn't care. Oh, dear."

She leaned as close to the window as she could, pressing her cheek against the screen, but Ginger had disappeared. Not for worlds would Patty get up for an unobstructed view above the kitchen counter. It made her more miserable to sit hunched up, watching the narrow strip and Ginger's back door.

But Ginger was out of view so long. Patty could imagine her sitting on the grass, jabbering away to Spark Plug, perhaps even to five or six other boys. And at last she could stand it no longer. She had to know what was going on beyond her line of vision, so she got up and went to the big wide window. She tiptoed over, as if Ginger might hear her.

But the yard was empty. Only Spark Plug's two little sisters galloped by, hitched to a piece of rope and playing horse.

She's inside, eating the fudge, Patty thought miserably. The whole gang's probably in there, playing records and eating. And she leaned across the counter to fold her arms on the sill and rest her chin on them, patiently watching and waiting. They were bound to come out *sometime,* and it was better to know what she was missing than to blindly wonder.

But Spark Plug's back door opened suddenly and only Ginger shot out. She carried the blue bowl and was quite alone. And as she ran down the steps she kept her head up, looking—as she had been looking for the last three days—at the back of the Palmers' house. Patty, standing in a frame, tried to duck back. Her foot slipped, her chin bumped the window sill, and she flung up both arms to save herself. She couldn't bear for Ginger to catch her in the undignified act of snooping.

But Ginger saw only the upflung arms. Patty was waving to her! Patty was *actually waving!* "Hi," she called, and began to run.

And now what to do? Patty collected herself and stood uncertainly, rubbing her chin. Ginger was coming. It was what she had wanted her to do, but it meant that an apology would have to be made face to face instead of into the impersonal mouthpiece of a telephone. She wished she hadn't promised to tell Ginger that she was sorry she had behaved so badly. She wished she could hide. She wished Ginger would turn around and go back, or would even stand still until she could rehearse a polite little speech. Cool, dignified, was what she would be. Then the door burst open and she and Ginger were hugging each other.

The blue bowl banged against the back of Patty's head and sent words tumbling out. "I'm sorry," she mumbled. "Oh, Ginger, I am—I am. I know you're my friend, and I'm sorry."

"Oh, pooh. Forget it." Ginger stepped back and grinned. She had whacked Patty with the bowl again, so she set it on the counter and said, "You're the one who had to miss the fun."

"Was it a very good party?"

"Oh, so-so." Ginger thought it would have been a bang of a party had Patty been there, but she said, "You didn't miss much. Wouldn't your folks let you go?"

"Hunhuh." Patty had more she must say, and she hung her head. "They didn't like the way I treated you," she said. "They told me I'm—horrid and—and spoiled."

"Well, I guess you are." Ginger laughed, and added, "And I guess you knew it before they said so."

"Yes, of course I did." It felt good to drop off part of the heavy pack of misery she had been carrying around, and Patty drew in a deep breath of release. Ginger knew the worst about her now. She had confessed. "I wish I could be more like you," she said, letting her breath out in a sigh.

For Patty to admit her faults, even one or two, was so amazing that Ginger felt a little giddy. She vibrated between pity for a friend who had had a hard time—and who would still have it if she persisted in carrying the torch for Tim—and exultation because Patty, for once,

110

had admitted to being wrong and had removed the blight of blame. Ginger wondered how long she would remain starred in the spotlight of admiration, and decided not long; so she tried to put it to use while she could.

"I'll tell you what," she said bravely, seeking a chair for assistance, and looking up at Patty, who still stood uncertainly by the door where they had bumped into each other. "It's sort of up to you. If you can stop believing that Jane and Betsy and Phyllis know everything, and can stop thinking it's important to have a steady date to carry your books and hang around you, nobody's going to hash this over. They'll forget it."

"You mean. . . ."

"Yes, I do." Ginger watched Patty's big blue eyes grow wide from lost confidence, but went sturdily on, "You can't make Tim go steady, Plus, you just can't do it. His father told him he couldn't—and he's not about to buck his father. And I'm not about to get squashed in the middle again," she added, standing up for herself so staunchly that her mother and father would have been proud, could they have heard her. "Tim's swell. I like to have him around, and so does Spark Plug. But Spark Plug made him go home yesterday afternoon because he can't stand quarreling. That's what he said."

"I didn't know that." Patty leaned against the counter and ran her finger around the circular stripes on the bowl. "I thought. . . ."

"I know you did," Ginger interrupted again, since Patty's thoughts were almost like her own. "That's why Tim called you. He wanted to make peace with Spark Plug and the rest of us." And then she stood up. "If you

111

want to be mad at me again," she said, "you'd better say so right now."

"I don't want to be mad." Tears of shame pushed against Patty's lashes and the stripes blurred. "I want," she said, looking up humbly, "to—to have you all like me."

"Oh, Plus, we do." Ginger jumped up and shut her heart, tight, against Patty's crying. "How about going over to Spark Plug's?" she suggested eagerly. "He's going to work on Beauty for a while."

"He wouldn't want me."

"Of course he would. Bill Templeton's coming, and Steve. Oh, Plus," she cried, swallowing her happiness because this day had come right, "Mom's promised me a puppy. Maybe Spark Plug will drive us out to my Aunt Margaret's and we can choose it. Maybe he will. And we can take a picnic and eat it in the pavilion over the brook. And we can bring the puppy home with us, and it'll be such a lot of fun. Oh, please, Plus."

"All right, if Mother and Daddy will let me." Patty wiped away her tears. Her acceptance was reluctant because she knew she had been an interesting topic of conversation for the past three days. "Do you think Tim will be there?" she asked hesitantly.

"Nope—and what if he is? You aren't going to bite each other, are you?"

"I hope not."

Patty tried to smile, and Ginger went on eagerly, "He's the one who started talking about the puppies and made me want one. So if he goes along, who cares? I almost hope he will, so we can be a regular crowd again. Not that Spark Plug's in the crowd," she added, drawing her mouth down with what she hoped was a comical look. "But he does like to drive our station wagon and he's nuts about the machinery Aunt Mag keeps in her barn, so he may take us. Why don't you go and ask your parents, while I set things up on my end of the line?"

"Perhaps you'd better ask them. They're—they're kind of mad at me."

"Okay, where are they?"

One more courageous act wouldn't matter on this day of days, but Ginger was relieved to hear Patty say, "Next door, at the Cummings'."

"Then I think I'll just leave a note," she decided. "Give me your mother's grocery pad." And she scribbled:

We've kidnapped Patty. We're going out to my Aunt Mag's—we hope—and if you want to know more about it, just call up my mother. And after a moment of indecision, she signed it, *Patty's best friend, Ginger.*

"I guess that'll explain to them," she said, not wanting to waste another precious second. "Come on. You can comb your hair and put on lipstick at my house. I'll lend you a sweater."

The quarrel was over, life was about to begin again, and Ginger was so happy that she dragged Patty down the back steps, forgetting the bowl she had left on the counter.

Chapter 9

Patty was chatty enough, crossing back lawns, but when they reached Ginger's steps she hung back. "Did you tell your mother about me being mad at you?" she asked.

"Natch." Ginger went on ahead and held open the screen door. "Mom couldn't help seeing that something was wrong," she said. "You weren't over here and I wasn't at your house, so I had to tell her why. She won't hit you."

"What about your father?"

"He's a good egg. Come on in before fifty million flies do."

Ginger shooed away September flies that were already seeking a warm retreat, and Patty reluctantly climbed the steps. "I don't want to see either one of them today," she said uncomfortably. "If they're as cross with me as Daddy and Mother have been I'd rather wait for you in the kitchen. You go on in and tell them you want to borrow the car and I'll wait for you here."

But Ginger's mother pushed open the swinging door at that moment and looked inquiringly from one to the other. "Well," she said, "I see that you two have made up."

Her eyes lingered longest on Ginger. Ginger had been

114

sent next door with a bowl of chicken, and back she came
with Patty. It was the mud-pie episode all over again. The
gullible child giving in to the smart one. And she was
relieved to have Ginger say, "Patty waved to me from her
kitchen window, so I went over. She was awfully lonesome."

"You see, Mrs. Johnston," Patty spoke up, "my mother
and father wouldn't let me go to the party." Apologies
came hard to her, but she made a valiant effort to assemble
a few well-chosen words. "I shouldn't have blamed Ginger
because people don't like me."

"Oh, honey." Katherine Johnston reached out to hug
Patty, forgivingly, lovingly. "You're a dear little girl,"
she said, "and we're all very fond of you. All children
have to be punished once in a while, you know."

"I deserved it." Even in her embarrassment, a shim-
mering halo hovered over Patty's head, and she let it come
down to rest on her curls as she said, "Ginger's always so
good. She never cares if people mistreat her, or worries
about being unattractive. I suppose I shouldn't have so
much pride."

Mrs. Johnston turned her attention to Ginger, who
had been made to sound like a moron. Ginger looked as a
girl should look, on Sunday. Her hair was combed, her
plaid cotton was—due to Ginger's having sat so still all
day—practically unwrinkled. But she did look, as Patty
had said, "so good." There she stood, ready to march on
beside Patty again. And, Mrs. Johnston thought ruefully,
summing it all up in metaphorical style, Ginger would
carry Patty's banner while Patty smiled and bowed to the
people. An almost unbearable tenderness flooded her
heart, and she wanted to shake Ginger awake, then hug

115

her. But she only smiled at Patty again, and asked, "What are your plans for the rest of the day?"

Ginger's tongue was the one that started going. Ginger was the one who said she'd die if she didn't see the puppies today, who coaxed to borrow the new station wagon, and finally came to a stop by saying, "Simply gobs of boys are coming over to Spark Plug's and we can take them along."

"Only if Spark Plug drives," her mother gave in, when Ginger was about to fall on her knees and continue her supplications from there. "He's the only one your father will trust."

"Oh, thanks, Mom, thanks in bunches." Having had one wish granted, Ginger was quick to present another one. "If Aunt Mag has any puppies left," she begged, "may I bring one home tonight?"

Ginger didn't look as if she needed the puppy, now, but an offer was an offer, so Katherine Johnston stayed with it. "Oh, I suppose so," she said. But she warned, "Don't be hopeful. Aunt Mag has five puppies and dozens of friends. Will you be home to supper?"

"Ummm—I don't know." Ginger was on her way out but she stopped to say, "We might throw some picnic stuff together if Spark Plug will go, or we might stop somewhere for hot dogs and malteds. I might kind of throw a little party," she suggested hopefully, "if you'd like to advance my next week's allowance."

"And you might kind of not. No advance. Now run ask Spark Plug, so your father and I'll know what to do about our own transportation."

Ginger led Patty out into the sunshine again. Patty dreaded this next meeting far more than she had the last one because she often felt uneasy and strained with Spark

116

Plug. She wilted under his scowl and could never talk to him as Ginger did, sometimes squabbling with him, sometimes saucy, and often meek.

"I hope he won't turn us down," Ginger said, leading the way. "If he does, I'll have to threaten him."

"With what?"

Patty knew of no hold that Ginger could possibly have over anyone so honest and girl-shy as Spark Plug, so she was surprised to hear Ginger say, "With Daddy's car jack. Spark Plug's crazy about it and Daddy lets him use it. Beauty's tarpaulin belongs to us, too."

"Why don't you go in by yourself and ask him?"

Patty stopped at the Blakes' back steps while Ginger ran on up and looked through the screen. "Hey, you," she called, seeing Spark Plug moving about inside, "we're going out to Aunt Mag's, and Mom says you have to drive us."

"How come?" Spark Plug appeared at the back door, a thick sandwich in his hand. "Maybe tomorrow," he halfway promised. "I'm busy today." Then he saw Patty looking up at him. "Hi," he said; and she could only smile feebly.

"But it has to be today," Ginger insisted, cutting off his solemn regard of Patty and bringing his attention back to her. "Aunt Mag goes to business tomorrow, so I have to get my puppy today." By now she thought she owned one, and she pleaded, "Oh, Spark Plug, I just have to have it. It's so lonesome at our house without a dog, and Mom and Daddy want one, too. Believe me, if I knew of any other way to get out there, I wouldn't ask you."

"Thanks." He took another bite from his sandwich and considered her thoughtfully while he chewed. "Tim,

117

and Steve, and Bill, are coming by," he said at last, "and Tim will have Mary Lou in tow."

"Oh, that's all right." Ginger brightened visibly, and offered as the victor, "If my Aunt Margaret doesn't invite us to stay out there for supper, I'll bring the whole gang back home with me." She grinned down at Patty, and predicted happily, "This is a good way to get started again."

Patty wasn't so sure. Not with Mary Lou in possession of Tim. Mary Lou was apt to balk at taking a drive with an erstwhile rival. She was good-natured, but she also was fat. She gave parties in her fine, big house, she organized clubs and helped run the sophomore class, but it was a rare occasion when a boy stopped by and asked her to go somewhere. "I'd better go home," Patty said.

"Now, Plus." Ginger hurtled down the steps, leaving Spark Plug to think what he liked. She coaxed Patty, she praised her, and she was scolding, "I don't see whatever became of your self-confidence," when Mary Lou and Tim came around the side of the house.

They looked surprised when they saw Patty, but they kept on coming, so Ginger ran to meet them. "We're all going out to Aunt Mag's to get me a puppy!" she called. "Just as soon as Steve and Bill come. Spark Plug's going to drive our station wagon, and we'll have supper somewhere, so you'd better telephone home. Come on, hurry!"

She left Patty enough time to haltingly explain to Mary Lou again about why she had had to miss her party and to go home for the gift she had bought. Then she hustled back to her house for the sweaters and coats they might need.

Mary Lou good-naturedly helped her find a box for the

puppy to ride home in, but she snatched the privacy to ask, "What gives with Patty and Tim?"

"Nothing. They've just decided to be like the rest of the gang—that's all."

"Couldn't she really come to my party?"

"Hunhuh." Ginger threw an old quilt in her box and called good-by to her mother and father. "She really did have to stay home," she said, pushing Mary Lou outside ahead of her. "Parents can be an awful nuisance, can't they?"

"But I'll bet she still flies the flag for Tim."

Mary Lou remained unconvinced, so Ginger had to mention Phil Lebensdorfer. "Not since she had a date with a cousin of Bonnie's," she said, pitching the box and sweaters into the back of the station wagon. "He's a real fire-boy."

She was glad to see Bill Templeton lounge out of Spark Plug's back door. He was usually with an older crowd, and was good-looking in a hewn-from-a-granite-block way. He had the build of a football player and was as dedicated to athletics as Spark Plug was to old cars. Girls played a small part in his life, but he was accustomed to having Ginger around, so he climbed into the seat she assigned him in the car and said, "I was sorry to have caused your brush with old Stillman. How did you come out?"

"Oh, just fine." Ginger had a hostess's job on her mind. She also had a delicate situation. So with Bill next to Spark Plug and herself on the outside, she put Mary Lou and Tim in behind them. That left Patty and Steve to ride backward in the third seat, facing the tailgate. Steve looked acceptant and Patty unhappy, but she herded them in. "I think we're ready," she said, "so let's go."

119

Fortunately, the station wagon was long, and those spaced so far apart were seldom in conversation with their neighbors. Bill and Spark Plug talked, Mary Lou and Tim kept up an earnest conversation, and Ginger couldn't hear what Patty and Steve were saying, so far behind her. She simply rode along in happy silence, thankful to be where she was, and thinking about the puppy she would bring home.

"Mom said she'd tell Aunt Mag we're coming," she turned around to say, when they pulled up before an old stone and clapboard farmhouse. "If you want to go out in the woods and hunt for walnuts, you can. I want to see the puppies first."

"So do I." Steve pressed a button that lowered the tailgate and gallantly helped Patty out. He was younger than the other two boys and had never got over the wonder of having Spark Plug let him hang around, so he added, "Unless I can help park the car, or something."

"We'll leave it right here in the driveway." Ginger was off in a flash. She knew the puppies lived with their mother in an annex that was called "the summer kitchen," and she ran around the house with the others trailing behind.

Mary Lou was not overly fond of her own big dog that always followed her brother, so she loitered along with Tim. Patty was doing her best to hang onto Steve and hold back Bill, keeping a boy on each side of her, so only Spark Plug caught up with Ginger.

"Do you really want a puppy?" he asked, when the others had stopped to look down into an old stone-walled well and wind up a bucket of clear, cold water.

"Why, sure. Why not? You have a dog."

120

"He isn't any good. He just stays in the house all day."

"Dachshunds do." Ginger gave a skip, and said, "If Aunt Mag gives me a dog, I'll feed him and play with him, and make him really mine."

"He'll just be a miniature poodle, and that's not much bigger than a dachshund."

"I know it." Ginger laughed and pushed open the door to a low-ceilinged room.

Puppies waddled to her from all directions. Their mother, lying in her basket, growled a warning to them, then recognized Ginger and got up, wagging her short pom-pommed tail. She was a beautiful dog, and she was proud of her curly black offspring.

"Hello there, Folly," Ginger said, stooping over to run her fingers through the dog's topknot of curls that stood up on top of her head like a round black biscuit. Folly continued wagging, so she sat down on the cool stone floor and let the puppies scramble into her lap.

"Which one is yours?" Spark Plug asked, holding out his hand for Folly to sniff, as a stranger should when making friends with a dog.

"I don't know. I don't even know if Aunt Mag has any left," Ginger admitted. "I'm only hoping."

"And you dragged me all the way out here—for *this?*" Spark Plug's voice that had been a deep bass for at least two years broke in a shattered falsetto. "Well, my gosh," he said, pulling it down to its proper level, "I could have stayed home and worked on Beauty."

"I knew that." Ginger grinned up at him. "You wouldn't have come if I had hung a 'maybe' on," she wisely told him. "Now, would you?"

"You bet your sweet life, I wouldn't."

121

The door opened again for Steve; and before Ginger had decided which was the puppy she had liked best, the others had come in and were bending over them, too, expressing their own personal opinions.

"I'd like to have this one, if our cat wouldn't kill it," Patty said, cuddling a black fluffy ball against her blond curls, then holding it away to smile at it. "Let's take this one, Ginger."

Ginger looked up. The puppy, should she be so fortunate as to acquire one, would not be a joint ownership deal. It would be hers and hers alone, and there would be no sharing of the leash when she walked it to town. The one who fed and trained it would walk behind its stylish prancing. She was about to make that clear when her Aunt Margaret came in.

"Hi, kids," she said breezily. "I heard you were coming out to look at my babies. Down, Folly."

She was a large woman, as tall and heavy as her sister was tall and slim, and her iron gray hair was cut short and brushed back from a round intelligent face. She was the comfortable tweedy type, and she radiated pleasant good-humor. "What do you think of them?" she asked.

"Oh, we adore them," Patty breathed, still holding the one she had chosen for Ginger and herself.

"They're cute," Steve added, not knowing that Ginger's ownership was in doubt. Which one is Ginger's?"

"Well, now let me see." Margaret Partridge had had a telephone conversation with her sister, and she looked down at Ginger, sitting with the biggest, fattest puppy on her lap. "I've promised them all," she said, "except the one I'd planned to keep. Now where is he?" She studied each little face intently before she looked down and said, as if surprised, "I believe you're holding him, Ginger. Would you like to have him?"

Ginger had been silently stroking the puppy while she did some thinking. She loved him. She loved him dearly—but he had such a beautiful home here. He and his mother had acres and acres of fenced-in ground to run about in. "He's darling," she said, "but I can't take him away from you, Aunt Mag. It wouldn't be right."

"Oh, nonsense, child. If you want him, take him."

"Oh, I do." Ginger stroked the puppy from his black little nose to his stump of a wagging tail as she tried to explain, "I do want a dog. I'd love one the way some girls can love brothers and sisters—and I've missed Blossom, you know. But, oh dear," she sighed, "this is your dog."

"You can have him, honey."

"No, I can't." Ginger kissed the puppy and held it up. "I've been sitting here thinking about it," she said. "This precious baby has a better home than I can give him—being in school all day and not having any other pets around—while there are other dogs who don't. I think I'd rather leave this one with you and go to the pound and find some lonesome little pooch. There's bound to be a puppy there that needs me. It probably wouldn't have a pedigree like Folly's children, or be as beautiful, but it wouldn't have a home, either. Thank you, Aunt Margaret, but I'll wait and go to the pound."

Miss Partridge wondered what Ginger's parents might say to this new development. Of her six nieces and nephews, Ginger, because of her thoughtfulness and loving heart, was her favorite. She understood Ginger. "I think that's a good idea," she said, accepting the puppy and full responsibility for whatever Ginger might do. "This one does have a home, as you say. There's an A.S.P.C.A. boarding kennel and shelter near here, if you want to drive over and look. I'll round up a picnic lunch in the woods while you're gone."

"I don't know." Ginger looked up at Spark Plug. "I didn't expect to go today," she said. "Do you think we could?"

"Sure, if you want to," he answered gruffly. "You and I might go alone, if the others don't want to."

He was proud of Ginger, but he didn't intend to let her know it. And he wanted to help her select the dog, but not with the others along. Too much advice was always confusing, and the whole business was up to Ginger, anyway, he reasoned. So he said, "We'll be back in a little while," and asked Miss Partridge for directions to the Shelter.

Patty didn't want to go. Just any old dog wouldn't be as cute as the one Ginger had refused, so she went out into the sunshine. Bill had two hunting beagles at home and it was his job to feed them, so he went with her. Steve had never cared for pets, Mary Lou wanted to stay where the crowd was, and Tim got a warning shake of the head from Ginger.

"What kind of a dog do you want?" Spark Plug asked, when they started off alone; and she shrugged.

"I don't know," she answered. "I'd like him to be pretty, but it wouldn't matter too much. Just so he's pleasant. If I can find one, I think I'll choose a little wooly dog that's sort of cozy. The frowzy, Teddy bear type, you know."

They drove along a winding country road, and as the

Shelter was only a few miles away, its gate was still open and an old attendant was sitting beside a tree.

"Sure, we got dogs," he said, in answer to Ginger's eager inquiry. "All kinds. Want to see 'em?"

"Oh, please."

She and Spark Plug followed him through an office and into a long cement-walled wing that made Ginger think of the cell blocks she had seen in movies. Cages were built three high along the walls, and at the sound of the opening door meows and barks poured from them. "We keep all the cats on the top row," the man said, moving along swiftly. And Ginger closed her eyes to keep from looking at them.

Some of the cages were empty, but he stopped before one where a black and tan German shepherd pawed at the wire. "This is a handsome feller," he said. "His owner got jailed for embezzlement, so we picked him up this morning. He's worth five hundred dollars, and a friend of the guy's said he'd be over for him tomorrow, but you can take him if you want him."

"No, not if he can get a home," Ginger said, moving on to the next cage where a Doberman sat. She didn't much care for Dobermans, but the dog looked lonely. "What about this one?"

"Well, I'll tell you," the old man said, taking off his battered hat and scratching his head. "I kind of promised him to my nephew, if he's still here by nightfall—but I don't reckon I ought to hold him if you like him."

Ginger moved on. Two dogs were promised, a mother and three puppies were being boarded until their owner came back from a trip. A collie had been found that morning and its frantic owner had telephoned in. The next

dog was so old and so sound asleep that it didn't open its
eyes. Ginger stood looking sadly at it until a whimper
from across the aisle turned her around.

A tan and white puppy had his white front paws
through the screening and his fat stomach pressed against
it. He was calling her as best he knew how, and she knelt
down before him. "Oh, baby," she cooed, "are you lonesome?"

He wept that he was. Life had been unkind to him, he
told her, jumping up and down and trying to reach her.
He had lost his mother somewhere, and a man had
brought him here. He wanted out.

"Could I hold him?" Ginger asked.

"Sure. Just pull back the bolt."

Spark Plug watched Ginger kneel down and cradle the
frowzy, wriggly little dog. "What breed is he?" he asked.

"I don't know." The man shook his head. "Collie and
German shepherd, I'd say. He's got good points, but
they're mixed."

"How old is he?"

"Ummm—maybe two, three months. He's going to be
a big dog when he grows up to his paws."

Ginger had wanted a small, cozy dog, and here on her
lap was something that might grow to the size of a horse!
She was wiping away smears made by a tongue that was
already longer than Folly's, and she said, "Oh, dear. Does
anyone want him?"

"Not so you'd notice it." The attendant leaned against
a cage and said indifferently, "He's been here eight days
and his time's about up."

"What does that mean?"

She looked up at him, waiting for his answer, and he

shrugged. *"Pffft*—the gas chamber," he said. "We can't keep 'em forever, you know."

"I'll take him."

She got up with the puppy still hugged to her and turned her back on other cages along the row. "Don't show me any more," she said, swallowing a lump in her throat. "I might want them, and I can't take them all. Do you like this one, Spark Plug?" she asked.

"Sure. He's better than the one I have." Spark Plug held out his arms to carry the puppy for her, but she shook her head.

"He has to learn that I'm his owner," she said. "If he knows I chose him and am going to take care of him, he'll stay with me better. Am I supposed to sign for him?"

"Nope," the old man answered, snapping the lock on the empty cage. "I'll just write him off on the books. You want a rope to tie around his neck?"

"I'll buy him a collar and leash tomorrow."

Ginger hoisted her wriggling burden higher and tried to tuck a thumping spike of a tail under her arm. She was beginning to worry about what her parents might say, and she looked doubtfully at Spark Plug. "He'll need all kinds of shots," she said, remembering what her Aunt Margaret always did for her dogs. "I hope they aren't dreadfully expensive. Do you think Mom and Daddy will mind?"

"Search me," he returned, scratching the puppy's head as they walked back to the car. "They said you could have a dog, didn't they?"

"Yes, but not this one. Mom likes French poodles because they don't shed, and Blossom had short hair. She wasn't very big, either." Ginger shifted again to see where she was going, and pulled her face away from the puppy's pink tongue. "This one is apt to be enormous," she said, stumbling over a stone in the parking place, "but I love him. I feel tender, already."

"You can bring him over to my house sometimes." Spark Plug opened the car door and tucked the wagging tail in before he closed it again. "What do you think you'll name him?"

"I haven't thought about it."

"Let's call him Butch."

"Oh, *no!*" Ginger kissed the top of the puppy's head, then set him upright on her lap. "He's too sweet for that kind of a name," she said, "and he's going to be pretty. I'll have to wait and think of a name."

"Okay." Spark Plug climbed in and started the motor. He drove along while Ginger pointed out the sights to her darling, and every now and then, too, he reached out to tousle the small rough head.

Chapter 10

A telephone call from Margaret Partridge had prepared Ginger's parents for the mongrel puppy they were to welcome. But even so, when the front door opened and a bundle of tan and white fur bounced across the living room rug, they had to laugh.

The puppy cantered in in a series of sprawling leaps, then fell over his feet. He sat up to look at the strange people who confronted him like two enormous statues, hung out his pink tongue and gave a feeble wag of his tail, then started to cry. Where was his darling?

"I'm right here, baby," Ginger said, shedding her sweater as she came. And, picking him up and cradling him under her chin, she asked confidently, "Isn't he darling?"

"He's going to be a man-sized dog," her father answered, pleased. "The kind that comes bounding across the lawn with the evening paper in his mouth."

"The kind that knocks everything off the coffee table with one sweep of his tail," his wife retorted. "But he is cute. What are you going to name him, honey?"

"I haven't decided." Ginger put the puppy on her father's lap, proudly watching the brave way he accepted stroking from a strange hand. "The whole crowd thought up all sorts of names," she said, "and Spark Plug kept calling him Butch. I'll have to wait to decide."

She went off to hang her sweater in the coat closet, and the puppy landed on his chin when he tried to scramble down and follow her. Wherever she went, he was right behind her. To the kitchen and back, to the bedroom and back, to the kitchen again. He was tired from so much trotting about but he kept on going, and when Ginger went off to find an old basket that would do for his bed, he staggered sleepily to his feet and followed. "Wait for him," her mother called. "Wait for your shadow."

"That's it!" Ginger stopped in the dining room, and cried, "That's his name—Shadow. Hi, Shadow."

"Come here, Shad, old boy," her father said, promoting the small fat creature to adulthood. And he grinned when Shadow turned and gave an answering wag of his tail. "By golly, he's smart," he said proudly, remembering Blossom who had been dear, but too timid and shy. "He knows his name already. I'll treat him to a collar and leash tomorrow."

"He'll have to have distemper shots, and hepatitis shots," Ginger counted on her fingers, remembering the list of costly things her Aunt Margaret had said a puppy would need, "and rabies shots, and a license, and wheat germ, and cod liver oil. And he ought to have a real basket, like Folly's, and a little plaid overcoat for when it gets cold. Oh, my, he's going to be awfully expensive."

"I'll drive you around after school tomorrow," her mother promised. "We'll take him to Doctor Burnside's, then buy whatever you want. But no overcoat," she added, laughing at her husband's unhappy expression. "Daddy would be ashamed of a dog in an overcoat."

"And Shadow would be embarrassed." Ginger laughed, too, and went off to hunt the basket, even though she knew that, for his first night at least, Shadow would curl up on the foot of her bed.

She fed him again and took him out for a romp on the lawn, then settled down to her homework. The puppy lay on her desk, biting her pencil and giving her wet happy kisses whenever her face came close to his. It was companionable, and she was sorry when the telephone rang.

"Hi," Patty said, when Ginger had rushed in to sit on her mother's bed, leaving her puppy crying lonesomely on the floor. "Phyllis called up and asked us to be on her committee for the Halloween dance decorations. I'm in charge of decorations, and you're in charge of food, and she wants us to meet at her house tomorrow. She can't have us in the afternoon, because of Hal, you know, so she wants us to come for a while after dinner. Hey—are you listening?"

Ginger was upside down, comforting Shadow, who had to learn that all beds except hers were taboo, and she straightened up to say, "I heard you, but I don't think I can make it."

"Why not?" It popped into Patty's mind that Ginger probably had a clandestine date with Tim, so she asked again, "Why can't you come?"

"Because of Shadow," Ginger answered. "My puppy I mean. I named him Shadow."

"What's the matter with him?"

"Nothing. I just ought to stay home, that's all. Everything's so strange to him, and I can't ask Mom and Dad to. . . ."

"Oh, gosh," Patty interrupted. "Phyllis asked me to be

on one of her committees, and I suggested you for the other one. I did it for *you!* And now I suppose you're going to be tied to that dog forever. I think it's silly."

She was to repeat that again and again as September moved warmly on and October took its place. Shadow was Ginger's constant companion. He frisked about Spark Plug's yard, he trotted in a wavering path on his fine red leash when Ginger held the end of it, and sat down and had to be dragged when anyone else held it. He slept at her feet when she took him to the drugstore, or squeezed into the crowd around the juke box with her. He became everybody's pet, and Patty complained one day:

"It's no fun going places with you any more. Everybody fusses over Shadow."

"You mean Tim does." Tim had brought Shadow a silver name tag and they had spent an hour on Ginger's back steps, clamping it to the little dog's collar and tossing him his ball, just to hear the cheerful jingle it made against his license tag and his rabies disk. It had sounded like a charm bracelet. And Ginger said now, "I should think you'd be grateful to Shadow. All the boys come to see him and you get to walk him."

"Only when you're along," Patty returned grumpily. "He won't move without you."

"He just doesn't understand about a leash yet, that's all. If you'd be patient and try to coax him. . . ."

"I don't want to. I think it's silly just sitting around every afternoon, oohing and gooing over a dog."

"You've had some dates out of it," Ginger reminded. "Bill walked over to your house with you and Shadow yesterday, and Steve asked you to go to the movies Saturday night, and you're going out to Aunt Mag's with Tim on Sunday."

"So are you and Shadow."

They were sitting in Ginger's kitchen that day, waiting for Shadow to finish his early supper, and Patty went on disconsolately, "We're only going out so your aunt can check up and see if you're doing everything right for a dog. I never heard of anything so stupid. You're worse than a *mother!*"

"But we're taking Tim's car and you'll get to sit beside him."

"Who cares!" Patty glared at the little dog, who had stopped trying to lick the enamel off his bowl and now lifted his head to grin at her. "He's not so bad," she conceded; "Shadow, I mean, but I do get awfully tired of him."

There were times when Ginger got tired of him, too, but she didn't say so. Shadow still had to be taken outside every half hour, and he didn't like to sleep as late as she did. He had chewed her new pumps and eaten her library book, but he was so cute and loving that the work of bringing him through puppyhood was a pleasure.

She hurried home from school every afternoon, leaving Patty to stay or go on as she liked, and Mrs. Johnston was pleased. Ginger was crawling out from under Patty's thumb at last! But one afternoon she came into the kitchen and gave the ecstatically dancing puppy such a perfunctory pat that her mother was afraid she and Patty had quarreled again. Mrs. Johnston thought she couldn't go through another drawn-out quarrel.

"Mom," Ginger said, sitting down and not noticing

that Shadow was chewing the toe of her loafer, "I'm awfully worried."

"Oh, mercy, child," her mother sighed. "Not again."

"I guess I told you that Mr. Stillman's wife is sick,"
Ginger went on, looking up, her eyes filled with sorrow.
"Well, Miss Maxwell says she's had her operation. I've
been asking about her, and I feel so awfully sorry for Mr.
Stillman."

"Why, darling? Is he sick, too?"

"No, but. . . ." Ginger leaned over and picked up
Shadow. "He's having such a hard time," she said, pushing the puppy's face away, then kissing the top of his head.
"Miss Maxwell says he has a woman to stay with his kids
during the day and while he runs over to see his wife in
the hospital, but she goes home about five-thirty and he
has to fix his own dinner, put the children to bed, and
work on his next day's lessons. He's got so awfully thin
and nervous, and I don't think he's eating enough, poor
man."

"What do you think you could do, dear?"

"I don't know." Ginger fluffed up Shadow's raggedy
curls and said thoughtfully, "I guess I told you about the
day he got mad at me, didn't I?" And at her mother's
nod, she went on, "Well, we've become awfully good
friends. I always ask him how his wife is, and he asks me
how my puppy is, and we make little jokes together. You
see," she said, "nobody else in our class likes him. He is
sort of scary," she admitted, "but he's worried. He doesn't
know many people in this town, and he's plain tired, and
hungry, and worried."

"Would you like me to make an extra tuna fish casserole

tonight—the one that has all the vegetables in it—so you can take it over to him?" her mother asked.

"I wouldn't want him to see me." Ginger rested her cheek against the puppy's cold nose as she explained, "It's considered apple-polishing to give special presents to teachers—except Miss Maxwell. Everybody loves Miss Maxwell. And I wouldn't want Mr. Stillman to think I'm trying to *make* him give me a good grade. Do you suppose," she looked up to ask, "that I could sort of leave it on his back steps, then run away?"

"You can try. I'll drive you wherever he lives, and be ready to pick you up and whisk you off. I wonder. . . ." It seemed foolish to worry about losing one of her glass baking dishes, but Katherine Johnston went on, "How I can get my casserole back."

"Oh, I'll write him a note and stick it under the lid. I'll tell him to put the dish out in the morning so I can leave him another one at night." Ginger looked up, her face so bright and relieved that her mother hadn't the heart to ask how long she would be cooking for two families. She thought that Mr. Stillman might tire of baked dishes, but Ginger went on, "The things I take him can be sort of filling, and I can vary his diet with chops now and then. His mother-in-law is coming as soon as his wife gets home from the hospital, so he'll be all right, then. Miss Maxwell says the poor woman has a job and can't come any sooner. I'll pay for whatever we send out of my allowance."

"Oh, darling." Mrs. Johnston bent over and kissed the crooked little part in Ginger's bright hair. "I'm ashamed that we older people haven't thought of helping him," she said. "Our church should have done something."

"I guess he hasn't gone to church yet, with his wife sick,

and all," Ginger answered. "They just came, you know, and he's awfully proud and cold to people. Shall we take something to him tonight?"

"If you like."

Ginger hustled about to help with the baking. She and Shadow went down to the basement for more cans of tuna, she walking down the steps and he falling most of the way, and she resolutely kept her eyes turned away from Spark Plug's yard, and her ears closed to Patty's laughter. But later Spark Plug saw her come out with the glass-topped dish.

"What you got there?" he asked, moving from his driveway to hers.

"I'm taking something for somebody's supper. It's a present Mom made."

"I'll drive you." His friends had gone and most of his tools were put away, so he ambled on to her station wagon and opened the door.

"Well—my mother was going to do it," Ginger answered haltingly, embarrassed to have him know she was leaving Mr. Stillman's supper on his doorstep. "That is, she said she would, and she's coming with Shadow."

"Get in." Spark Plug drew himself up on his toes and said through the kitchen window, "I'm taking Ginger because Mom wants you to come over and see a new hat she bought today. I said I'd tell you." Then he swung himself behind the wheel and asked, "Where does this character live?"

"Oh, dear. Well—it's Mr. Stillman," she blurted, since there was no way to keep him from knowing. "And you'll have to wait while I go get Shadow, and then keep him in the car and park down the block so he won't see me—Mr. Stillman, I mean. It's—it's sort of a surprise."

"Okay."

That was one of the nice things about Spark Plug, she thought as she ran back to the house. He never asked questions. And he was never surprised at the strange things other people might do. His mother complained about it sometimes, and said she pitied the girl he married, but Ginger thought it was a very comfortable way to be. Now he simply hoisted Shadow onto the front seat and started the motor.

"I think he lives near Mary Lou somewhere," Ginger said, getting in.

"I know where it is."

They rode along in semisilence, with Shadow the target for what conversation there was. He pawed at the savory-smelling food inside the glass dish and, failing to get at it, wanted the penciled note fluttering out from under the lid. And when Ginger held the dish too high for him to reach, he tried to help Spark Plug drive.

"This is the block," Spark Plug said, slowing down, "and that's Stillman's house over there on the left. What do you want me to do?"

"Stop here." Ginger looked across at a small box of a cottage. It had no porch, and rolled newspapers on the steps told her that the closed front door was rarely opened. "He'd never find it there," she said, wishing the house had even a few bushes and trees around it to provide cover for her trip to the rear. "I'll just walk on the lawn next door, then sneak across to the back steps."

"Want me to do it?"

"No, I guess I'd better. Mr. Stillman might come home

and you'd have to drive off. You watch and I'll hurry. Take care of Shadow."

She slid out of the car and crossed the street, walking softly, as a burglar might. She felt like a burglar as she hugged the back of the house and leaned across narrow brick steps to set the dish before the door. She could hear a child crying and water running, so she knew the small Stillmans were having their baths. What if someone should come out and step on the dish? she worried, moving it to one side, then setting it back again. From the looks of the yard, Mr. Stillman wouldn't bother to pick up anything he could walk around or step over, and he might not notice anything so small and out of place as a casserole. The water was still running somewhere near her, so she hoisted a small tin wagon up on the steps and put the dish in it. "There!" she mumbled. "Try to get around that!" And she took off at a run.

"What made you so long?" Spark Plug asked, when she tumbled into the car again.

"I couldn't find a good place to put it."

Ginger started to comfort a lonesome, disconsolate Shadow, but Spark Plug proved that his mother could sometimes be wrong about him and that he did have a bump of curiosity tucked away in his skull by asking, "How come you're feeding old Stillman and being so anonymous about it?"

"I feel sorry for him," she said simply, as brief as he usually was, "but I don't want him to think I'm trying to get better grades in Latin, that's all."

"How long're you going to keep it up?"

"Till his wife comes home from the hospital, maybe a

week or ten days. I do wish," she said with a sigh, "that I'd thought of it sooner."

"I'll bring you over when you have to come." Spark Plug turned the car around, and asked generously, "Do you think I ought to add some ice cream for the kids, or something?"

"No, the woman feeds them, Miss Maxwell says. It's just Mr. Stillman I'm worried about. But it was nice of you," she added, "to suggest it."

"I'll quit work early every afternoon and clear out the gang in time for us to get here before the old boy shows up," he offered. "What did you say in the note?"

"Oh, just. . . ." Ginger stopped and grinned. Spark Plug was showing such an unusual interest in her affairs that she changed the grin to the nicest smile she could give him. Of course he didn't see it, with his eyes straight ahead on the traffic, but she leaned around her puppy and said, "I just wrote, 'Please put the dish out in the morning and look for another surprise every night. Happy days.' And I signed it, 'A friend.'"

"Why did you put 'happy days'?"

"I don't know. I just wanted him to be happy, that's all."

"Well, I'll bring you back tomorrow."

Ginger and Spark Plug ran their catering service for five days, undetected. Ginger picked up her empty bowl, or plate, or pan, each evening and replaced it with a full one. She wasn't certain, but she thought Mr. Stillman looked better. He wasn't any fatter, she decided, studying him critically each morning, but he wasn't so gaunt, either. And he certainly was more pleasant. He even tried to joke with the class, in a pathetically stilted way, and was almost jovial whenever another teacher came in. Then on Friday afternoon, at the end of school, he called her up to his desk.

"Ginger Johnston," he said, when she was filing out to go home with Patty. "Will you wait, please?"

"Yes, sir."

Ginger's eyes signaled Patty to go on; but, out of Mr. Stillman's sight in the hall, Patty drew down her mouth and clasped her hands together in a good-luck gesture. She pitied Ginger, but she hurried on.

"What is it, Mr. Stillman?" Ginger asked, walking slowly to the front of the room.

"Ah—er. . . ." He looked soberly at her and waited until she had reached his desk; then he smiled. "Happy days," he said.

"Oh, goodness." Ginger clutched the edge of the desk and turned white under her sprinkling of freckles left over from summer. "Oh, my goodness. How—how did you find out?" she quavered.

"The woman who takes care of the children happened to look out yesterday—just happened to, you understand, not curious—and she saw a girl about your age running away. After that, it was simple."

"It—it was?"

"Of course." He opened his desk drawer and took out one of her weekly tests and the note. "Do you see any similarity in the handwriting on these?" he asked. And she nodded dumbly.

"It was a beautiful thing to do, Ginger," he said, sliding his chair back and smiling at her. "My wife wants me to thank you. I've been the greatest part of her worry, you know—getting me fed and keeping me fit. I wish you

140

could see how much better she feels, just knowing I can sit down to a good, hot meal every night."

"I'm so glad, Mr. Stillman."

"I'm not much of a cook, you know, even if I had the time," he went on, "and Mrs. Garfinkle's contract doesn't include feeding me. The kids eat their big meal at noon and have cereal at night, so. . . ." He stopped and smiled again, such a nice grateful smile that Ginger wanted to cry. "My wife's going to get well," he said, his voice shaky with happiness. "She's going to get well, Ginger."

"Happy days," Ginger said softly. "I knew you'd have happy days, Mr. Stillman."

"That's what my wife says. You know," he leaned his elbow on his desk and regarded her with a glint of humor in his grave blue eyes as he said, "I'm about as poor with words as I am at cooking, and when I telephoned Mary last night—she's my wife, and she wants to know you, by the way—when I asked Mary how I ought to go about thanking you, she said, 'Why, just say whatever comes into your heart.' 'Happy days' were the words that came."

"Oh—my." Two tears did try to push out then, but Ginger blinked them back. "Golly," she said, "I won't have to sneak around to your back door now, will I? I can come later, when you're home."

"You mean you'll still keep coming?" he asked, surprised. "I can count on eating till Monday?"

"Of course."

Ginger wondered what Monday was to bring, and she listened eagerly while he said, "My mother-in-law gets here from California on Monday. She's a whiz. She'll have Penny and Pogo whipped into line and the house ship-shape by the time I bring Mary home, on Wednesday. I want Mary to know you, Ginger."

"And I want to know her, too, but mostly I want her to know my mother." Ginger beamed, wanting happiness to go on and on for the Stillmans. "Mom's the one who does the cooking at our house," she said. "And, Mr. Stillman," she, too, leaned an arm on the desk to say, temptingly, "we're going to have pork roast tonight. You weren't going to get that, because it won't be done in time, but if you can hold out until sixty-thirty, Spark Plug and I'll bring your plate over. Hot, you know. Spark Plug is Elston Blake, and he always brings me."

"Is he your boy friend?"

Mr. Stillman's twinkling eyes made Ginger blush, but she said, "Oh, mercy, no! He only lives next door, but he's nice. We'll have a good hot plate for you."

"I'll tighten my belt till then."

He dropped his hand to pat hers and give it a squeeze. "If my Penny doesn't grow up to be as considerate as you are," he said, "I'll whale her within an inch of her little life. Now, run along. Have fun, and give your mother my grateful thanks."

"I will. Happy days."

Ginger walked along the hall and down the ramp in a dream. Patty was still waiting for her outside the door, and she asked, "What happened? Did old Stillman blast you?"

"Hunhuh," Ginger answered, thinking that Miss Maxwell would be a good one to gather a crowd of young adults together for the Stillmans.

"Well, what did he want?" Patty persisted.

"Nothing much." Ginger snapped her mind back to

142

the present. Patty had stood on the steps a long, long time, patiently waiting for her best friend who might be in trouble again. That was unusual for Patty, so she said, chuckling a little inside, "He'd been comparing one of my tests to some other stuff he had. And do you know, he *liked* what I'd written!"

Chapter 11

"Mom says I can have a party," Ginger told Patty on Saturday morning, standing on the back lawn and watching Shadow drag a rope over grass that was beginning to grow just a little tired and ready to sleep. "She doesn't approve of birthday parties with presents," she went on, forgetting that Patty had just had one, "so she said I can have mine now, while the weather's good. I've been thinking about what kind I want."

"Would you like a slumber party?" Patty asked, remembering how exciting and sleepless hers had been.

"Hunhuh. Nope." Ginger shook her head. "I thought about it a lot, last night," she said, catching the end of Shadow's rope and laughing at his growls that were supposed to sound fierce. "You've been having dates with lots of boys, haven't you?"

"Just Steve." Patty tried not to sigh or look at Tim, who was in Spark Plug's yard, as usual, as she added, "And that dumb Phil. Why?"

"Well. . . ." Ginger threw the rope back to Shadow and sat down on the bottom step. "I've been thinking I might have a hay ride," she said. "You missed the one our club had last year."

144

"Oh, *would* you?" Patty flopped on the step, too, and pleaded, "Oh, Perse, *do it!*"

"I want to," Ginger explained thoughtfully. "Mom called up Aunt Mag and she says she'll send a wagon for us, not a truck. The flat kind of wagon, with real horses hitched to it, and bells on them. And she says she'll fix all the food, hot dogs and stuff, to eat in the woods, and Mom and Daddy'll give it to me for my birthday present."

"Oh, Perse, please, *please* do it!"

"And I've been thinking," Ginger went on, saving the best for last, "that maybe Tim ought to take you."

"Oh, no." Patty drew herself up and declared, "He wouldn't want to. He'd rather take you."

"I don't think so." Ginger knew that Tim would take Patty if she told him he had to, but she only said, "You've been going to parties with other people, and he sort of hangs around you. He does do that, doesn't he?"

"Sometimes." Patty was embarrassed, because she had made a silent vow to win Tim back. She wanted to do it without Ginger's help; but, she reasoned to herself, a little boost wouldn't be exactly helping. Given a chance, away from Ginger, Spark Plug, Beauty, and the ever-present Shadow, she could make Tim sorry that he had cut himself adrift in a lonely world. "All right," she gave in, "I'll go with him if he asks me to. When will you have it?"

"Next week end. Friday or Saturday night. Wait a minute, I'm hungry."

Ginger went inside and returned with two pieces of cold fried chicken. "Which one do you want?" she asked, holding them out.

"I don't care."

Patty reached for the breast, so Ginger munched on a

drumstick. "If the weather looks good for Friday," she said, feeding bits of her chicken to Shadow, who promptly left his rope to paw at her knee, "we'll have it then. That gives us a chance to postpone it to Saturday night, if it rains."

"Will you go with Spark Plug?"

"I don't know." Ginger laughed and tried to hide the bone behind her. Shadow's eager little nose found it, so she said, holding it above her head and ducking his lunges, "I may just go with my boy friend here."

"Oh, you aren't going to take *him!* Oh, don't. Leave him at home," Patty begged.

"I can't. Mom and Daddy will be out there, too."

"Then let him ride with them in the car." Patty could see the hay ride turning into a shambles with a small dog climbing over everyone. And since Shadow never knew who liked him and who didn't, he was apt to settle himself on her lap—or worse, on Tim's. Tim would play with Shadow and ignore her.

"He won't bother you," Ginger promised. "I'll keep him up beside the driver and me. If he's going to live in our family," she said, "he has to learn to go everywhere we go and be a good sport. He's already learned to stay in the car and not cry. Now, Shadow, calm down."

She took Patty's clean-picked bone and her own, and went inside again. Patty reached back to open the screen door enough to let Shadow through, too, then got up and strolled across to Beauty. "Hi," she said to two pairs of feet.

Tim looked out but Spark Plug stayed hidden. "Check the grease on the differential," was all Spark Plug said.

"I'd better get Ginger to come out and work the gears for us. Something's slipping."

"I could do it." Patty was eager to sit on the high seat in an important role, but Spark Plug's grease-smudged face appeared.

"She knows how to," he said, sliding out for an oil can, which she pushed toward him with her toe. "Run get her." Then he called as she started off, "Tell her to bring the box of candy with her."

"What box?" Patty put on her brakes. "I haven't seen any candy around," she said.

"The box I gave her last night. Maybe she hasn't opened it yet."

"I didn't see it."

"That's funny."

He hoisted himself to a sitting position and directed his voice at his living-room window. "Hey, Mom," he shouted, bringing his mother into a frame of ruffled white curtains. "Did you buy that candy for Ginger when you went to the drugstore last night?"

"Oh, Elston," she answered contritely, "I'm sorry but I forgot it."

"Well, that's just dandy. My gosh," he grumbled, glowering at her, "can't I trust you? You were supposed to buy it and take it to her when you and Dad went over to play bridge."

"Listen, my son." She rested her elbows on the sill and pressed her forehead against the screen while she said, "I'll give you a few pointers on etiquette. Any young gentleman who desires to present a box of candy to a young lady proceeds to a store and makes his purchase.

147

Then, box under arm, he rings the young lady's doorbell
and. . . ."

"Oh, nuts." Spark Plug grinned and waved her away.
Then, before she could leave, he called, "What did you
do with my money?"

"I still have it. I'll give it to you when you're ready to
go to town."

Tim and Patty looked at each other. Patty shrugged
and Tim grinned, but Spark Plug cut into their silent
exchange of glances by saying, "Don't be so smug. This
isn't romance. Ginger did something that I thought was
swell, that's all, and I thought I'd reward her by *buying*
candy, instead of letting her cook it. Anybody want to go
to the drugstore for me?"

"I could, I guess." Patty hoped that Tim would offer
to drive her but he was crawling under the car again, so
she said with a little prick of conscience, "It isn't exactly
fair to buy Ginger a box of candy, then make her bring
it out here so we can all eat it. I wouldn't like that, if I
were Ginger."

"Okay, so she doesn't get it."

He started banging away with a wrench, and Patty
peeked under the car to suggest, "You might buy it later."

"I might."

The morning wore on, and candy wasn't mentioned
again. Patty didn't want Ginger to hope for something
she might never receive, and Spark Plug and Tim forgot
it.

Ginger sat in the car, working levers when told to and
planning her party with Patty. But when the noon whistle
blew at the fire station, and the others went reluctantly
home to lunch, she got out and sat on the running board.

"Hey! There's a man parking a Cadillac in front of your house," she said, watching the street, "and he's looking back here."

"Uh." Spark Plug only grunted, sitting in the driveway and bolting two rods together.

"He's coming around the house," she reported. "Maybe he's looking for you. Oughtn't you meet him and ask him what he wants?"

Spark Plug glanced up then, and his heart stood still. He laid down the rods he was working on and got up, wiping his grease-stained hands on his coveralls. This was the one man in town who might want Beauty—just as she stood. "Hello, Mr. Clivesdale," he said. "How are you?"

"Fine, thanks. That's quite a car you have there."

"Yes, sir."

Kent Clivesdale was a youngish man who liked old cars. He owned several but was always looking for more, and he had the money to buy what he wanted. "I heard you'd bought this," he said, taking off his felt hat and wiping a florid forehead with a monogrammed handkerchief, "but I thought it was a Maxwell."

"No, sir," Spark Plug answered. "It's an Overland, with a Continental motor. This is Ginger Johnston, Mr. Clivesdale."

"How do you do." Kent Clivesdale turned his attention back to Beauty, walking around her and carefully inspecting each inch. His keen blue eyes studied her headlights, the square lines of her hood, the open wires where a taillight belonged. "You still have a good bit to do," he said.

"Yes, sir," Spark Plug answered. "And she'll get a paint job."

"I like to tinker with cars, myself. The sport of having an old one is fixing it up and making it run. This one isn't as old as I'm looking for, but I could do a lot with it."

"I'll have to go," Ginger said hastily, backing away from the stricken expression on Spark Plug's face. "Good-by, Mr. Clivesdale." And she went running across her own lawn.

"Oh, please, don't let him take Beauty away from Spark Plug," she prayed, standing by her back steps, her eyes squinted shut. "Not yet. Don't let him offer so much money that Spark Plug will think he has to take it. Let him have some fun with her first. Let him keep Beauty until he's ready to sell her."

She didn't hear Shadow scratching at the screen door, refreshed from a nap and wanting to come out and play; she didn't hear her mother in the kitchen; she only stood with her eyes closed and both hands pressed over her mouth.

"Ginger?" her father said. "Lunch is ready." Then he opened the door and came out. "What is it, honey?" he asked, going down the steps to take her hands down and search her face.

"It's Spark Plug," Ginger groaned. "A man wants to buy his car—before he even gets to finish it, Daddy. A Mr. Clivesdale. Do you know him?"

"Yes, he's president of the Clivesdale Magneto Company," Stuart Johnston answered. "His father built the company up and now Kent runs it. He already owns two or three old cars, so are you sure he wants Spark Plug's?"

"He likes to restore them, he said. Oh, Daddy," she wept, picking up a ball and throwing it so Shadow would

150

stop jumping up and down against her, "do you think he'll offer Spark Plug so much money that he can't afford *not* to sell Beauty to him?"

"Honey, I don't know. Do you want me to go over and find out? I might talk with Spark Plug's father."

"Oh, Daddy, *would* you? Quickly? Before Spark Plug gives in and says yes?"

"I'll try."

She watched him saunter away, exactly as if he were going to the Blakes on some unimportant errand, then dared to walk to the corner of the house and peek around it. Mr. Clivesdale was still looking Beauty over. He looks at her as if she were a thoroughbred in a ring, Ginger thought, and he's judging her points.

And Spark Plug still wore his same stricken expression. He looked even more blank and numb than he had when she had left him, and she ducked back out of sight. "Please, please, please," she whispered her prayer again, leaning against the side of the house to wait.

It seemed an endless time before she saw Spark Plug walk back to his garage, carrying his tools. It looked so final. Beauty must have been sold, if the tools were being put away right in the middle of a Saturday.

She couldn't see Spark Plug's face, but his shoulders slumped. He wasn't standing straight and whistling. "Wait a minute," she called, running toward him.

"Oh, hi." He stopped and turned around then, and waited.

"Did—did you sell Beauty?" she asked.

"Not yet. Dad came out and said we ought to think it over. I don't know, though."

They went into the garage and he put his tools in a

special cabinet he had built on the wall, while Ginger stood and watched him. He put them in so slowly and with such loving care and finality that it made her heart ache.

"I could just about pay for a couple of years of college with what he'll give me," he said, padlocking the door to the cupboard. "It seems foolish not to take it."

"What did your father say?" Ginger asked.

"Oh, while Mr. Clivesdale was poking around, he called me inside and pointed out that really old cars don't grow any younger. Your father was there, too, and they kept telling me that Beauty will get more valuable as time goes on. I buy that," he said, testing the lock, "but I need the money. My folks aren't rich, you know."

"They *want* to send you to college."

"Oh, sure. They want to send the other kids, too." Spark Plug leaned against the wall and said gloomily, "Dad's been staking me to car parts ever since I bought Beauty and quit working in the hardware store, the advance being his stake in her sale. I don't know anybody but Mr. Clivesdale who might want to buy her. I ought to sell, Ginger."

"Not yet." Ginger felt very brave as she said, "If Daddy thinks you should wait, and your father thinks so, too, it's right to follow their advice. Why do you suppose Mr. Clivesdale came here today?" she asked. "He knows what Beauty'll be worth when she's finished. How dumb can you get?"

"I don't know. I'm all mixed up."

He walked out of the garage with her beside him, and said, "I don't feel like working any more today, somehow. I wish there was a football game, or something."

"There isn't one till next week."

"I know it. Maybe I could go down and work in the bowling alley. Styx is always offering me a job." He became conscious that she was still beside him—the good little friend. "I'll tell you what," he said, looking out at the sunshine splashed over Beauty. "I gave Mom some money to buy you a box of candy last night—for being so nice to Mr. Stillman, you know—but she forgot it. I guess we could go down to the drugstore and buy it now."

"I don't want to." Ginger shook her head in positive veto. "I'd rather use the money for a new glass in Beauty's taillight," she said. "I really would."

"How come? Do you mean that?"

"Sure, I do."

She smiled at him and was glad to see him straighten up—so tall that she had to look up at him. Confidence had come back into his eyes, and he said, "You don't want me to sell Beauty, either, do you?"

"Not yet. There aren't many Overlands to be had," she explained. "I've heard you say so. And I don't think you should grab the first offer that comes along. If you do, you're slipping."

"Thanks, pal."

He whirled around and left her standing there while he went back and unlocked his tool cabinet again. He was whistling happily now, taking out the wrenches he had just put away; and when he had what he wanted, he called, "You go eat a quick lunch, then you can go with me to get the taillight fixed. Bill owes me sixty cents, but he's gone off with the team."

Ginger was about to say that she had a dollar and a half saved, then decided that the price of a box of candy was a large enough loan for one day. "Can Shadow go, too?" she asked.

"Sure, if you put his leash on. Tim'll be back and you can ask Patty. But keep her out in the car. She's no good in a machine shop."

He was whistling again, so she walked on home. "Big afternoon," she told Shadow, who hadn't seen her go into the garage, so thought he had lost her forever. And she explained about Beauty's near sale to her mother, who was worried in a different way.

"I've been trying to keep the hamburgers hot," her mother said. "One minute you were in the side yard, the next minute you weren't. One minute your father was right here in the kitchen, the next minute he'd disappeared into thin air. Really, Saturdays around this house try my patience. Patty called you. Steve did, too, and Mary Lou, and some girl who must have been chewing bubble gum. I never did make out who she was."

"I need a secretary. Say, Mom," Ginger sat down at the table with her plate and recounted, "Spark Plug was going to buy me a box of candy—only his mother forgot to do it—so now he's going to take me with him to buy a piece of glass instead. Isn't he a laugh?"

Mrs. Johnston agreed that Spark Plug was positively side-splitting, and suggested that Ginger comb her hair and put on a fresh dress for a date with anyone who was so funny. "And," she said, "don't forget to be home in time to take Mr. Stillman his dinner."

"In *time!*" Ginger shrieked. "How long do you think it's going to take Spark Plug to run into a shop and order a round piece of glass?"

"If he's anything like your father," her mother retorted,

"once he gets in a place like that he may never come out. I've spent hours waiting for just a little piece of plywood to be cut. Machinery and males must magnetize each other. Now, run along."

Ginger dressed carefully, and thought she looked as neat as Patty when the two of them sat on the back seat of the Blake sedan, waiting for Spark Plug and Tim to come out of a dull-looking shop.

"Mom was right," she said, after the first hour of waiting.

She and Patty had discussed the hay ride until each felt that she had gone on it and come home again. Patty had agreed that Beauty should be kept until they had had some fun with her, but she thought Ginger had been foolish to give up her box of candy, and vehemently said so.

"You don't get boxes of chocolates very often," she said. "I've never had but two from a boy, and one of those Steve gave me for Christmas. Can't you keep that dog quiet?"

"Hunhuh. He does better in our station wagon where he can run around." Ginger leaned over the front seat and pressed on the horn. It was hot in the car. The afternoon sun beat down and they were miles and miles from anywhere. "If I had a license to drive," she said, pressing her hand on the chromium ring and keeping it there, "I'd go on home and leave them. If they ever do come out, let's not speak to them."

"All right. Here they come."

The door to the factory opened, and the neglected two on the back seat arranged themselves in silence. Patty pretended to be asleep, and Ginger sat straight up and held Shadow. But neither Spark Plug nor Tim seemed to

155

notice. They got into the car discussing a headlamp they had seen, repaired for an old model T Ford, and were back home before Spark Plug looked around and discovered them. "Gee whiz," he said, "I forgot we had you."

"You did not." Ginger got out and stalked away. "You were just being horrid," she said over her shoulder. Then she wheeled around and announced, with her hands on her hips, "I've changed my mind. I'll take the candy."

"Well, gosh—gee whiz." Spark Plug looked so taken aback that she was tempted to forgive him. His money— or hers, whichever way one cared to look at it—was gone, and he had a small piece of glass in his pocket. The sweet, indecisive Spark Plug she had known before lunch was gone, too, and she was left with this selfish, grumpy one she was used to. "Oh, all right," she said, giving in a little. "But don't you come around coaxing for cake. Let's go home, Patty."

Patty was undecided. She thought it would be a wasted Saturday afternoon if she spent it with Ginger, and was sure the long delay hadn't been Tim's fault. Spark Plug had been buying the glass. "All right," she agreed reluctantly, since no invitation to stay broke the silence. "But I do think," she said crossly, catching up with Ginger, "you might have waited a minute."

"Oh, we'll come out again," Ginger answered, stumbling over Shadow who was as loath to go in as Patty was. "Spark Plug'll call us after a while, on some excuse or other. Until then, we'll sit at the table and let them see us drinking lemonade."

"I don't want to." Patty followed her up the steps and walked over to the picture window. "I have pride, Perse," she said, as if she had just discovered it. "No boy's going

156

to invite me to go somewhere, then treat me just any old way. I don't see what became of all your personality that Doug said you had."

"Well, it's this way." Ginger took a pitcher of lemonade from the refrigerator, then closed the door and leaned against it. "I understand Spark Plug," she said. "Goodness knows, I ought to. And I like him. I feel sorry for him sometimes—his brain's so muscle-bound. I'm not trying to impress him," she said, shaking her head. "He's just Spark Plug."

"You can have him!"

Patty flounced into a chair and glared out the window. She didn't glare at Elston Blake, who had ruined her afternoon. She glared unwinkingly at Mark Timberlake Ford, the third.

Chapter 12

The days poked along for everyone who was invited to Ginger's hay ride, but at last the week rolled along to Thursday. The girls who had dates by then relaxed, some satisfied and others merely acceptant, but the ones who were still waiting for a boy to call them grew anxious and relied on Ginger to pair them off. Patty was among those.

"I don't know what to do," she said to Ginger after school, dumping her books on her desk. "I run every time I see Steve coming. If I do get left with him and he mentions the hay ride, I try to change the subject. I know he'll ask me because he thinks he has to, but I don't want to go on it with him."

She looked cross, and she sighed. "Steve's nice," she continued petulantly, "but I'm fifteen and he isn't yet. He's such a *child*. After you're fifteen," she informed Ginger, who was in no hurry to advance her age, "everything's different. You *feel* older. I'd rather go to your party with other girls than with Steve."

Ginger had done her best for Patty, with Tim. She had done it by praising Patty to him and letting Tim know that Spark Plug would sit between the driver and her. This, she knew would certainly happen, because Spark Plug would naturally take his place up front where the

158

activity was. She and Shadow could squeeze onto what was left of the seat. And since the hayrack would load at her house, Spark Plug and she would either get on together or he would haul her up when she told him to. She supposed she had a date. Spark Plug talked as if she had, so she asked Patty, "Do you want me to tell Tim to call you?"

"No. I think he's selfish and—smug. He hasn't asked anybody, because he thinks all the girls are simply panting for him to do it. Mary Lou and me, I mean."

"Well, gosh, Plus," Ginger said, sighing in sympathy, "maybe I should ask Phil Lebensdorfer at the last minute."

"Don't you dare!"

The telephone rang, and Patty, filled with hope, sped into her mother's room to answer it, while Ginger walked over to the window and wondered what to do. She could see Tim in Spark Plug's yard, so he couldn't be talking to Patty. Who was? Gasps and delighted acceptances were all Ginger could hear.

"Oh, I'd love to," Patty was saying, when Ginger stalked in to announce that she was going out to give Tim a piece of her mind. "I have a ticket, but I know that yours will be loads better. Mine's only in the sophomore cheering section, you know. . . . What? . . . Oh, of course I'll wait for you afterward . . . Hm? . . . Oh, I'd *love* to." A longer pause followed, after which Patty laughed softly and said, in a sugary, breathless way Ginger had never heard her use before, "Thank you, Bill. 'By, now."

The voice on the other end of the line clicked off, and she flung herself back on the bed, still holding the receiver clasped to her. "I have a date for the game," she breathed.

"With Bill Templeton?" Ginger squeaked. "Why, how can you? He's *playing!*"

"Right on the fifty-yard line," Patty dreamed on, her eyes wide and staring up at the ceiling. "Right behind the team. And I'm going to the drugstore with him afterward. Not the way we always go, in a mob, but with the *quarterback*. I'm going to your party with him, and I'm going to the game with him the next day!"

"Well, mercy-on-us-goodness-Agnes," was all Ginger could think of to say, and she had to sit down on a chair to do that.

"Oh, I'm so happy, happy, happy," Patty caroled, springing to her feet and dancing about the room. "An *athlete! The star of the team! A senior!* Oh, Perse, isn't it *wonderful?*"

"I guess so. Why sure." Ginger began to come out of her trance, and she said, "I didn't know you liked him."

"I didn't think I dared to. Good gracious, Perse," Patty stopped dancing to expound, "you don't go around being ga-ga over an *athlete*. He's not like Spark Plug or Tim. He's *important* in school! I used to envy you because you could talk to him."

Ginger wondered when Patty had become tongue-tied with Bill. As far back as she could remember Patty had kept her starry eyes for Tim and had overlooked Bill completely. "When did all this start?" she asked.

"The day we walked Shadow over to my house, I guess. I just love Shadow!" Patty cried. "Let's go and get him and take him over to Spark Plug's."

"But Tim's there. What if *he* decides to ask you to

come to my party with him?" Ginger was practical. She
should have been home to look after Shadow long before
this, but Patty's need for comfort had seemed more important than another hour of her mother's time. She had
never thought of Shadow as a matchmaker, but she listened to Patty rave:

"He is the darlingest dog—I just adore him. And I do
hope Tim does ask me! I'll simply love turning him
down." She began twirling around and around, her skirt
flying out like a bell, her arms widespread. And when she
stopped, dizzy from spinning and from happiness, she
cried, "Oh, make Tim ask me, Perse! Do it any way you
know how, but *do* it! He *has* to ask me!"

"I'll try. It seems sort of mean, but I guess he does owe
it to you after fluffing you off," Ginger said, not knowing
she would make Patty's eyes blaze with such secret hate.
"I've never blamed you for being mad at him."

"I de-*spise* him!" Patty cried, with such bitterness that
Ginger believed her. "I've been lying awake at night
wondering how I could make him suffer. You've never
been fluffed off."

"Except by Spark Plug," Ginger answered, grinning.
"He fluffs me off all the time."

"And why should you care? Spark Plug's a square,"
Patty said, expressing an opinion that she supposed Ginger
must share, if she had any sense. "He doesn't do big things.
He's not an athlete. Come on."

Ginger got up and laid the telephone back in its cradle.
Patty had no more need of it now, but the rest of her
family might have. Patty was planning ahead, and Ginger
listened to her babble, "I'm so happy I could burst. I'll sit
beside Phyllis and Jane at the game, and when we go to

the drugstore, I'll be right in the middle of the cheering. Just think—I'll be with the hero!"

"If we win," Ginger couldn't resist saying, wondering if she looked as drab as she felt, stepping over the back hedge while Patty skimmed over it. She was happy for Patty, but some of the unkind things she had said still rankled. "I shouldn't let her get me down," she told herself, going up her own back steps while Patty danced on toward Beauty. "Why should I care if she makes fun of Spark Plug? *I* know what he is, so why should I care what *she* thinks? I like to go to the game with Mary Lou and a crowd of girls. I'm not jealous—I know I'm not. So why should I feel so cross? I never felt cross at Patty before."

She got Shadow and went outside again, her eyes seeking Patty, who was laughing and flinging her curls about. Tim sat beside her on the grass, and only Spark Plug was bent over Beauty's motor.

"Oh, here comes Shadow!" Patty cried, holding out her arms to the puppy as if she hadn't seen him for weeks. "Come here, lambie."

Shadow, unpredictable and unaware that Patty needed to hold him like a four-leaf clover, bounced off in another direction, and Ginger silently applauded him. Then Patty looked up. Her triumphant smile was gone. Her eyes were filled with something Ginger couldn't define. Defeat? Acceptance of her status with Tim as it would be from now on? Ginger couldn't name it. She only knew that all her love for Patty came flooding back.

She sat down on the grass, too, glad that she loved Patty again, and the afternoon went by as so many other afternoons had, with talk and laughter, and with Spark Plug whistling at his work, the only one who didn't know that Patty had failed to even a score with Tim.

Ginger couldn't tell him, not even when she was helping him put his tools away, and he asked, "What's with Patty and Tim? Is that deal on again?"

"Nope," she laughed. "Patty thinks he's a spook. She was being pleasant to him, that's all."

"It was a funny kind of pleasantness," he answered, fitting each tool into its proper rack. "If I ever have a girl, she'd better not try to kid me along and act so silly. I don't see what any guy wants with a girl, anyway."

"Mercy, I don't either—with a boy friend, I mean."

"Are you planning to ever get married?"

"Someday. Aren't you?"

"Ummm—I don't think so." One hammer was a little out of line, and he squinted as he straightened it. "Mom says there isn't a girl in the world who would put up with me. She says I'm low-level. Do you think I treat you all right?"

"As far as I've noticed." Ginger shrugged and moved another tool to give the hammer more room. "I think we're pretty good friends," she said. "Why don't you rearrange the pliers? Put the little ones in the middle and the big ones outside?"

"It might work better. I'll take them out and you hold them, then give them back to me the way you think they should go."

They had had a serious discussion, but only Ginger was aware of it. She always learned about Spark Plug from the remarks he let slip. She knew that he was shy, self-centered, generous, unassuming to the point of anonymity, and as stubborn as a mule when he thought someone was trying to lead him. Now, she discovered—he was worried about his future love life. Spark Plug was afraid of girls.

"Well, I'd better go home and set the table," she said lightly, when the cabinet was locked. "I sort of miss taking Mr. Stillman's tray to him. It got me out of helping at home. But I'm glad his wife's out of the hospital and he's so happy. Doesn't it seem queer to be giving a party without having to get ready for it?"

Spark Plug hadn't had a party since he was eight years old, and he hadn't helped with the preparation of that one. A party meant dressing up and trotting out his company manners, and he liked "having the gang in" better. The hay ride seemed to be much the same sort of thing to him—no work, no commotion—so he asked in all sincerity, "What's there to do?"

"Why, an awful lot, but my Aunt Mag's doing it," Ginger said. "Mom and I are taking out the paper plates and cups and marshmallows tomorrow afternoon, but she's doing all the rest. You'll find out what a lot of work it is when you get there. I have to check the list tonight and be sure that everyone understands about the time." And she couldn't resist adding mischievously, "You wouldn't like to bring Mabel Adams, would you?"

"No, thanks." Spark Plug thought of saying that he was already linked with Ginger Johnston, but decided it was unnecessary. "Why don't you give her George Bates?" he suggested. "He's as dumb as she is."

"That's a thought. I'd ask you for more gems but I have to go now. 'By."

Ginger didn't see him again until the next afternoon, when a crowd began to gather in her yard at five-thirty. A long flat wagon, hitched to three pairs of sturdy farm horses stood at the curb. Guests, after greeting their hostess in what was more of a quick check-in, rushed out to inspect this unusual mode of transportation. The horses were fed so much hay from the wagon bed that they only nibbled at it with their lips, and the early arrivals who had climbed up on the rack got down and up again so often that the street was littered with hay. Ginger did her best to see that thirty-eight guests were properly paired off in couples. It was hard to do, for only those who were going steady stuck together. Phyllis clung to her Hal, Jane to her Fred, Betsy to her Chipper, and right in there with them was Patty, swinging hands with Bill. Tim, she noticed, was being devoted to Mary Lou.

"I think we're all here," she said, when her parents had driven off in the station wagon. "Let's get aboard. Hey! Sit down!" she shouted.

Nobody heard her. They pushed and shoved and shot hay into the air, and those on the rim of the wagon bed either fell off or jumped. The horses became excited and pranced up and down. The driver tried to calm them, the crowd whooped, and Ginger wished she had a megaphone.

Then Spark Plug, sitting where she knew he would be, on the front seat, stood up. *"Quiet!"* he yelled. "Sit down in the hay! *Sit—down!* Squeeze into a place and stay there! We're going! Stop scaring the horses—and *sit down!"*

It was amazing the way they managed to tuck their feet under them and make room. The whole cheerful mass consolidated into a bright bouquet, and the ones left standing in the street found space to climb onto.

"Aunt Mag said the rack could hold forty easily," Ginger said, when Spark Plug took Shadow, and then swung her up. "Hi, Mr. Hines," she leaned over to say to the young tenant farmer who was driving. "I haven't had a chance to speak to you. You've been awfully patient."

"My kids'll be wanting to do this, someday," he said, "so I might as well get in practice. Are we ready?" he looked around to ask.

A deafening shout answered him, so he slapped his three sets of lines and signaled, "Git-up!"

Cheery little bells on the horses' harness began to jingle, and Shadow gave short sharp barks of accompaniment. The crowd on the hay rack started to sing "Jingle Bells," even though the wagon had turned onto a by-road and was going through a blaze of autumn color, and Ginger smiled happily at Spark Plug. He was watching the way Mr. Hines spaced the lines between his fingers, keeping contact with each pair of horses, and wishing he could try it.

"I feel like I'm back in the old covered-wagon days," Ginger said, swinging her feet between the high seat and the floor. "Here I be, aridin' along with my li'l boy, headed for Californ-i-a. I plumb fergot my sun bonnet, Paw."

She wore plaid slacks and a sweater, but she pretended to smooth down an imaginary calico skirt as she said, "This is fine, Paw, ain't it?"

Spark Plug fell in with her nonsense. "Yore little boy is shore right purty," he said, patting Shadow's head. And Mr. Hines laughed.

They played the game for another half mile, then Ginger gave Shadow to Spark Plug to hold and swung her feet around so she could face the crowd in back.

"If anybody wants to change seats with me for awhile," she called, "say so."

She hadn't meant them to but her eyes came to rest on Patty. Not for worlds would Patty change, she knew.

Patty was squashed in beside Bill, her back pressing against Tim's shoulder blade, and Ginger knew that she wouldn't move for the moon and all the stars thrown in. But Tim would have liked to. So would many of the boys. Only courtesy kept them from speaking up. This horsepower which moved them along was as hidden from them as if it were under the hood of a car, and they yearned to see it in action. Surprisingly it was Mabel Adams who said, "If you'll all help me get to the front, I'd like to. We lived on a farm until a couple of years ago, and I'd love to ride on a wagon seat again. Do you think I can make it?"

They boosted her along, exchanging her for Ginger in the scrambled transfer, and as the wagon rolled on, other brave ones called for a turn. Boys jumped off the back and climbed on at the front, girls chose the overland route, and by the time they reached Miss Partridge's lovely lighted farmhouse, Ginger wasn't at all surprised to work her way back to her seat and find Spark Plug driving.

"Listen, everybody," she stood up to say, when the wagon had passed through a woods and pulled into a glade surrounding a hunting cabin. "Don't get off until you hear what I have to say. We're going to leave here at exactly ten o'clock. Even starting then, we won't get home till after twelve, so don't go wandering off and think we'll wait for you. We can't. The horses can't stay out all night, so anyone who isn't here will have to ride home in the station wagon. If you want to see the old mill, or the well, or the barns, do it now."

She climbed down and left them to scatter. Some went to the big bonfire in a cleared space, some ran inside to look at the cabin, others took off in the pale evening dusk

toward the mill, and only Mr. Hines was left to unhitch
his horses and lead them off for a rest in the barn.

Patty walked slowly away beside Bill. "What would you
like to do?" she asked, proud to have someone to enter-
tain. "The kids are dancing inside. Would you like to do
that?" Then she remembered his game tomorrow. Douglas
always rested before a basketball game, sending her on
errands for whatever his mother wanted and letting her
wait on him. She had always thought he used his game as
an excuse to escape his daily chores, but now she felt great
consideration for Bill. He would do a lot of running up
and down the football field tomorrow. "Perhaps you'd
rather sit down," she said.

"What for?"

"Why, because of the game."

"Gosh, that's not till tomorrow. We only had signal
practice today, and I've been sitting all the way out here.
"Let's walk somewhere," he suggested.

"All right, I'd like to. There's a dear little brook down
this path," she said. "I just love brooks. Sometimes we
come out here in summer and splash around in a pool that
Miss Partridge has had dammed up, and in the fall we
hunt nuts in the woods. We did that a couple of Saturdays
ago."

"Ginger told me. She asked me to come along, but I
had to go away with the team."

"Oh." Patty strolled along, her hands in the pockets of
her new red toreador pants, her suede flats patting the
soft, leaf-strewn ground. Fading western sunlight slanted
through the trees, and she stopped beside a large round
rock to say, "I'll be sorry when daylight saving time ends
and it gets dark early. Winter makes me sad."

"Why?"

He leaned against the rock and watched her shake her head. "I don't know," she said slowly. "Things die. Little animals get so cold and can't find enough to eat. People are poor and cold, too, and everything's so bleak that I always try to remember a line in a poem I read—'If winter comes can spring be far behind?' Sometimes I don't believe it."

"I didn't know you thought that way." Bill hadn't known she had such long eyelashes, either. And he waited eagerly for her to go on.

"Oh, I do. I think a lot, but I don't tell my thoughts to just anyone." Instinct told Patty that she had talked enough about herself to arouse his interest, so she changed the subject. "If I ask you something, will you tell me?" she said, moving on.

"If I can." The path had narrowed, and he reached beyond her to hold back an overhanging branch on a tree, but she stopped again.

"It's awfully silly," she said, turning and looking up at him. "But then, girls are terribly ignorant about a lot of things—football, for one. I don't want to be. If I'm going to watch you play tomorrow, I ought to know what you're doing, don't you think so?" And at his nod, she said, with a frown between her arched little brows, "I'd like to have you tell me why—when a player has to go over to one side of the field, or is run out of bounds—the referee always carries the ball back in again, and puts it down, just so."

"Oh, that's simple."

Bill began to explain a rule that she had heard her father and Douglas argue many times. Her father contended that the old rule was fairer, when a team had to

169

work its own ball back into playing position and use some headwork to do it. And at the end of Bill's careful instruction, she nodded and said, copying Douglas's argument, "I suppose it cuts down accidents and makes a faster game, doesn't it?"

"You're pretty smart. Is there anything else you'd like to know?"

"Only how you always manage to wriggle away from a tackle and can throw such wonderful forward passes, and run so fast."

Patty swept her long lashes up, and he thought she might as well sit down on the rock beside him while he told her.

It took quite a time, interspersed with her glowing tributes and eagerness to learn more; and before he had finished, Spark Plug was calling from the top of the hill, "Come and get it! Hur-ry, hur-ry, hur-ry. Come—and—get—it!"

"Just go over to Daddy for your hot dogs and a long stick," Ginger was telling everyone when Patty and Bill came into the firelight. Buns and salad and pickles are on the table, with pitchers of milk and hot chocolate." She thrust a paper plate and napkin at Patty, and whispered, "Where have you been?"

"Walking," Patty answered. "Oh, Perse, he's wonderful!"

"And he's going away to college, next year," Ginger returned flatly. "You'd better eat before the food's all gone."

She had other guests to see to, but even as she ran about, she noticed that Bill cooked Patty's hot dogs, and she roasted him dozens of marshmallows. They danced con-

stantly together after supper, too, and Ginger wondered
what Tim was thinking about it. When she had a chance,
she asked him.

They were in the cabin, skipping along in a square dance
that her aunt was calling. Miss Partridge scraped away on
a fiddle at the same time, patting one foot for rhythm.
"Swing your partners," she shouted; and Ginger said to
Tim, "It looks as if Patty's forgotten you."

"Yeah," he answered.

"Ladies to the center, gentlemen outside," Miss Partridge ordered, flatting a note in "Turkey in the Straw,"
and Ginger had to leave Tim. "Forward and back, and
make a bow." They met again briefly, and he grinned.
"Ladies left, gentlemen right," Miss Partridge sang out.
"Grapevine now till you come out right."

They reached each other again, and Ginger asked,
"Does it bother you, Tim?"

"Nope." He swung her around as he was ordered to do,
and danced her to the middle and back. "Patty's a good
kid, but dizzy," he said. "Will you dance the next real
dance with me?"

"If I have any breath left."

Ginger was laughing so hard she could scarcely answer.
Her Aunt Margaret was fiddling for all she was worth,
not bothering with discords, and Folly and Shadow had
set up a mournful howling. The music hurt their sensitive
ears, and having stood it as long as they could, they raised
their voices in agony.

"I'll take them outside," Ginger said, when the dance
ended abruptly. "Oh, mercy, it's five minutes to ten! We'll
have to get started. Hey, everybody!" she stood on tiptoe
to shout. "It's time to go. Time to—*go!*"

The hay rack filled more quickly now, because everyone knew where and how to sit. A few sweaters and purses were forgotten, and boys hopped off for them. The horses pawed the ground impatiently, Mr. Hines shook his lines, and they were off.

Someone started to sing "Good Night, Ladies," and they all joined in, waving to Miss Partridge and Ginger's parents, who were framed in the lighted doorway. " 'Good night, ladies, we have to leave you, now.' "

"Oh, golly, I wish it weren't over," Ginger groaned, down on the wagon bed beside Mary Lou. She had given her seat to Tim as a very special kindness, and she said with a sigh, "I wish it were five hours ago."

"Well you have one consolation," Mary Lou told her. "Everybody says that this is the best party any of us has ever given."

Chapter 13

"Oh, go away, Shadow," Ginger mumbled, yawning and burrowing into her pillow. It was the morning after the hay ride, and she murmured sleepily, "Go find Mom."

"A-wroof." Shadow had grown tall enough to rest his paws on the edge of the bed and to climb up. He felt fine. The little naps he had snatched during the party had kept him refreshed, and after a long dreamless sleep he was ready to go out and play. So he pressed one hind foot against the box spring, and was pawing his way up, when Ginger threw back her covers and scrambled out of bed.

"All right, you little monster," she said, tousling his head while she sleepily carried him along the hall to the kitchen. "You can have your bread and milk while I dress. Okay?"

"A-wroof," he barked in assent.

Mr. and Mrs. Johnston were having breakfast, and Ginger woke up enough to say, "Everybody said it was the superest party ever. Wasn't it fun?"

"We thought it went off fine," her father answered, accepting Shadow on his lap, so Ginger could push up the sleeves of her cotton pajamas and stretch. "As Spark Plug would say, you look 'beat up.'"

"Ummm. Back later." Ginger stifled another yawn and

173

pattered off, banging into the dining-room table and weaving a crooked path to her room.

But she looked wide awake and freshly showered when she came back in a full striped-wool skirt and a starched white blouse. "What gives for breakfast?" she asked. "And please don't say hot dogs. There were hundreds of them left last night, but I couldn't face one this morning. "Yum, cream of wheat," she answered herself, peering into her mother's bowl. "Has the pest eaten?"

"Long ago. Spark Plug was here," her mother said, "and he told me to remind you that this is his big morning."

"What big morning?" Ginger asked, puzzled because Spark Plug had failed to mention that anything unusual was to occur today.

"He didn't say."

"He might have meant the football game," Ginger decided, frowning thoughtfully. "But that isn't until this afternoon. I do wish that dumb lug would tell people what he's thinking. How can he expect everyone to read his mind? Now he has me curious. I'll be back in a minute."

She skipped out with Shadow following her, and went across to the Blakes' back door. "Hey, stupe," she called against the screen, shading her eyes to see inside. "Are you in there?"

"Yup."

Spark Plug came out eating an apple and looking so neat for a Saturday morning that she thought he must not have gone to bed last night. He wore the same well-pressed slacks, a blue shirt, and, of all queer things, a necktie. His hair showed the path of a comb, too.

"Well, well, well," she said, looking him over. "How come you're so dressy?"

"Big day, like I told you. Do you want to go along?"

"I'd be happy to," Ginger accepted, "if I knew where I was going. I don't want to look at the display of wigs that belonged to famous people, or go to the zoo, or to the police court. Almost any other place would do, so speak up, man. Where?"

"To see if Beauty can pass her inspection test," he answered, so seriously that she knew he thought he had told her. He told himself so many important things that he was always surprised when others didn't know what he was talking about. "I've done as much as I can on her brakes and lights," he explained, "and I think she can make it. Want to go with me?"

"Now?"

"Right this minute. But you can't take Butch, here. It wouldn't help me much if he bit an inspector's arm off."

"Or kissed him."

Ginger raced back to her house with Shadow, and didn't wait to eat her cereal. A banana, she thought, would be just as sustaining, and two would be more so. So she peeled one and went out taking large bites from it, in order to start the second one before Spark Plug took it.

"Well, here we go," Spark Plug said, already behind the wheel. "I thought Tim would show up before this, but he hasn't, so you can sit here beside me. Watch that door when you close it. I haven't had time to fix the lock, yet."

Ginger stepped up on the high running board and grandly seated herself. She knew that Spark Plug hadn't expected Tim to go with him, anymore than he had expected her to. He was nervous and dreaded going alone, that was all, so he was being condescendingly kind. It was his way of whistling in the dark. "I feel sure Beauty will pass," she said, to lift his morale.

"I wish I did. When the guy tells me to blow my horn, I'll have to reach halfway down the steering post for the button, so don't you lean over to watch me. Let him think it's on the wheel like a modern car," he instructed, taking the top half of her second banana.

"I'll remember. Anything else?"

"I don't think so. I put a switch on the dash for high-beam and low-beam and dimmers, and I'm almost certain that the lights are focused right. If the stop light works, I ought to be set."

They had five miles to drive, so Spark Plug practiced working the buttons and switches. Ginger, perched up beside him and feeling like a doll in a show case, watched the interested expressions on pedestrians' faces. Most of them had never seen a car of such ancient vintage, and they stopped to stare.

"What are you going to do with Beauty after she passes?" she asked, holding on for a sharp right turn. Beauty had no wheel suspension, so Ginger skidded against Spark Plug and had to pull herself back. She hoped Mr. Clivesdale had faded from the picture, and was glad to hear him say:

"I've just begun work on her motor. Ed Hack says I can work in his machine shop at night, and Clem Coppage told me I can move down to his body and fender works when I'm ready." He squawked his horn at a dog that fled for its life, and explained, "Clem has a sanding machine and painting equipment."

"Will you sell Beauty, Spark Plug?"

"Sure. What would I do with her in college?" he asked. "I'll advertise her in some magazine this spring. Wups, here we are."

A line of cars waited back of the garage which served as an authorized inspection station, and he pulled Beauty in at the end of it, easing her gently into place. People gathered around her, returning to their own cars whenever the line moved, but coming back again to admire her. Ginger thought Beauty looked bug-eyed with importance.

"Keep your fingers crossed," Spark Plug mumbled at last, when it was his turn to take Beauty up a long cement ramp that led into the cavern. "Maybe I should have waited another week."

The inspectors were interested in such a quaint contrivance. They wasted time while they admired it, and the mechanic who was responsible for passing lights and horns, said, "That's quite a car you've got there. Let's hear her beep."

"Oh, she can. She's simply wonderful," Ginger said, smiling and holding his attention while Spark Plug reached down for the inconvenient button and pushed it in.

"Okay, let's see your stop light come on." The stop light worked. "Emergency brake?" It caught with a thump.

"I don't see why you're so worried," Ginger said in a low voice, as they waited for the next test. "When you fix something, it's fixed. Stop frowning and looking so scared," she scolded. "Beauty's doing everything right."

"I wish I could be sure of it."

They got out on the cold cement and an inspector

climbed in. He grinned down at them from his high seat, then put the car in gear and moved forward. When he slammed on his brake, Beauty stopped with a jerk.

Spark Plug wished he could see which holes the man punched in the card that had Beauty's serial number on it. And when he was behind the wheel again, he wished he could tell if her headlight beams focused properly on a horizontal bar that was set in front of them. He wondered how he could endure waiting while an old man went into his box of an office and looked over the data he had.

"He's getting a sticker," he said, his hand clammy on the clumsy wheel. "It has to say one of two things—'This car did not pass inspection,' or that I'm okay. Can you see which it is?"

"Hunhuh." Ginger tried, but even when the man was pasting the bit of paper on the windshield his hands were in the way. "I think . . ." she wavered, sitting forward, ". . . that—oh, my goodness—we passed!"

Spark Plug was so nervous that his foot slipped off the clutch pedal as he pulled back on his gear shift, and Beauty gave a grinding screech. She took off with such a leap that Ginger, still not upright, fell against the dash.

"Well, my goodness," she complained, as they tore out of the driveway and stopped for a red light, "you darned near broke my neck."

"She passed! Wahoo! Wahoo!" He leaned out to stare at a little boy who was standing in the middle of traffic, looking up at them. "Run, kid," he yelled. "Run for your life or the mighty monster'll get you."

"Oh, Spark Plug." Ginger rubbed her neck and

laughed. "You scared him," she said, as the little boy ran for the curb. "Didn't you really think you'd pass?"

"You never know. Dad's brand-new car didn't, last year. And the old girl *runs*," he gloated. "Even with her distributor head held on with one of Mom's hairpins, she runs. Hot diggity dog!"

The light changed, and he charged on again, saying, "It might be fun to drive her to the football game this afternoon. You know, great tooting of horn and waving of pennants. I feel like showing the old girl off."

"Do you mean it?"

"Sure. She's got a license, she's got insurance, and she's got the prettiest little sticker you ever saw, so I think I'll drive some of the guys to the game. Sounds good—huh?"

Ginger didn't know what to answer. There were so many *I*'s in his sentence and so many "guys" wanting a seat. "I guess so," she said without enthusiasm.

"How about decorating her?" he asked. "With gold and blue crepe-paper streamers. Have you got any money?"

"Fifty cents." Ginger had known the money was in her skirt pocket and had planned to treat Spark Plug to a bottle of cola. She had even thought they might crack one over Beauty's hood, the way a sponsor smashes a bottle of champagne over the prow of a ship at its launching. "Here it is," she said, holding out the coin.

"Keep it. I'll stop in front of the shopping center and you can go to the dime store and buy the paper. Here's a quarter more," he said, twisting to feel in his pocket, "and here're two nickels. Get as much as you can."

"All right." He pulled into the curb and Ginger got out slowly, wondering if there would be a seat in Beauty for her. Steve, Tim, Pewee, she counted—Bill wouldn't be able to ride around town before the game—Art O'Donnell, and Spark Plug. Five. She could ask him. He might say he'd squeeze her in—and he might say he couldn't. It was better not to know. "Just go home," she told herself, "help decorate, and hope."

"I bought a package of each color," she said when she came out, offering him two pennies of change, that he said she could keep. "I think you'll have enough paper if you cut the streamers about two inches wide."

"What's wrong with you cutting them?" He had to pull away from a collected crowd of the curious; and when he was free of the curb, he asked, "Don't you want to be in on this, too?"

"Huh? You mean. . . ." Ginger slid around on the seat to face him. "You mean you're counting on *me* to go with you?" She cried. "I have a *seat?*"

"Well, of course, you have a seat! Gee whiz! I brought you with me this morning, didn't I?"

"Yes, but only after Tim didn't show up." Ginger's spirits were soaring so high that they almost floated out through Beauty's cracked roof. Riding in Beauty had been enough but it seemed that more good fortune was still to come, because Spark Plug was saying:

"When I want Tim, I call him up, see? When I want you I go over to your house and get you. How about asking Tim and Steve to help decorate and go with us? If you'd like to have 'em, that is."

Never had she been so proud. Or so happy. Or so excited. This was as near to complete triumph as she had ever come. And when they reached home, she tore into the house, screaming, "Mom! Mom! We're going to hang streamers all over Beauty! And we're going to the game in her—parked right beside the bleachers where the band sits. Will you take a picture of Beauty when we have her finished?"

"I'd love to, with my new color film."

"Steve's out there," Ginger rushed on. "He's a cheer leader, you know, and he's going to call up the coach and ask him to let us drive right in the gate and park by the band. Beauty has an extra horn—a thing called a claxon— and Spark Plug's going to claxon it whenever anything exciting happens. And Mom," she asked, with very little breath left, "what shall I wear?"

"How about your blue skirt and gold sweater?" her mother suggested, bracing herself for Ginger's joyous hug. "Is Patty going?"

"Oh, no, just me. The boys and me, that is. Patty has a date with Bill Templeton, but Spark Plug doesn't know it. He says I have to be the only girl. Oh, isn't it a shame," she said, after doing a thorough job of hugging, "that Shadow can't go? He'd look so cute, sitting up on my lap. Oh, well, he can help us get ready. Come, boy."

She whisked out, forgetting her scissors, then came back for them and the china cooky jar her mother held out. "I wish Patty could have some of the fun," she said, taking it. "Will you call her for me and tell her to come over and help decorate?"

"She telephoned while you were gone," her mother answered, and said she's washing her hair. Now, run along and stop worrying about other people, child. Patty doesn't want to ride with you. She's probably excited about her date with Bill."

"Okay." Ginger took off again, and was completely

happy, sitting on Beauty's running board and cutting paper for the boys to drape in twisted festoons.

"We might open up the bottom half of the windshield," Tim suggested, when she had nothing more to cut and was in the fun, too. "We can lay some streamers under it, then slam the windshield shut to hold them. How about you tying them to the radiator cap, Ginger?"

"I'm busy. I'm winding paper through the spokes in the wheels," Ginger called without lifting her head. "Get Steve."

Only a few minor setbacks wasted the decorators' time. Beauty needed water, so the whole arrangement that had been hooked to her radiator cap had to be taken off and retied. The crepe paper gave out and Ginger offered her treasured CHS pennant to fill in the gap, and she had to take Shadow home because he nipped at her beautiful wheels.

"We'd better be ready to leave at twelve-thirty," Spark Plug said, when Beauty was a sight to startle the blind. She had had her picture taken, her occupants had climbed in and out for Mrs. Blake's movie camera, and now it was almost noon. "The game starts at two," he went on, "and we have to get Steve there in time to start the cheering. Ginger and I'll drive by and pick you both up. Are you sure, Steve, that it's all right with the coach for us to come in?"

"It's all set." Steve had been in conference on the telephone, and he said, "We drive right in. I'll be wearing my white slacks and sweater, and Ginger says she's going to carry out the gold-and-blue color scheme, so what are you guys going to wear?"

"Why, I'm going like I am," Spark Plug answered. "I

look pretty good. I don't have to dress up crazy, do I?"

"Not if you don't want to," Ginger put in quickly. But knowing that he would want to do Beauty credit, she added, "You'll be the driver, you know, and I expect you'll show more than the rest of us—the top half of you, anyway—so why don't you put on your gold bowling sweater?"

"Okay. Tim, what are you thinking about?"

Tim got up from the running board, grinning sheepishly. "I was just remembering an old raccoon coat my grandmother has stored away in the attic," he said. "I was wondering if I have enough nerve to wear it."

"Oh, do!" Ginger hopped up and down, clapping her hands. "Wear it, Tim. It would be simply perfect with the kind of car we have, and you could get out and walk around in it. *Please,* wear it!"

"Okay, I will—if it doesn't smell too much of mothballs. She's got a pancake hat, too, that used to belong to Grandfather. I'll see if I can dig that out. Twelve-thirty?"

"On the nose. See you then." Spark Plug dismissed his crew and started inside to have his lunch, but he stopped to give Ginger a warning. "Now watch the time," he told her. "Don't get hung on the telephone, telling all your friends what you're going to do. You eat and dress, and come right out. Hear?"

"Yes, sir, no, sir, yes, sir." Ginger skipped home. She thought she skipped—but she might have run, or even flown. At any rate, she was suddenly there. She was dressed, she was eating, and before she knew it she was kissing her parents good-by.

"This is an unexpected treat," her father laughed, wiping a pink smear from his cheek. "Are you leaving home forever?"

"Silly." She kissed her mother next, leaving a fainter smear that time, then she kissed Shadow. "I feel bad about Patty," she paused in the doorway to say. "I never did anything exciting before without telling her about it." Her eyes clouded, and she asked, "Don't you think I should take time enough to telephone her? Just to be sure that she's meeting Bill?"

"Run, honey," her mother urged. "Spark Plug is waiting."

"All right. If I get a chance, I'll ask him to let Patty and Bill ride home from the drugstore with us. Patty would like that—but then again, she might not want to. Oh, well, good-by."

Spark Plug was picking up bits of crepe paper when she reached the driveway. He had on his gold sweater, praise be—and, oh wonder of wonders, she thought, his best navy blue pants. He really looked stylish.

"Well, here I am," she said, waving to her parents who watched from the window, and standing where she knew she belonged, beside Beauty's back seat. "Am I on time?"

"You're a minute early." He picked up one more piece of paper, left quite by accident on her side of the car, then swung open the cranky front door. "Get in," he said.

"You mean I'm going to sit up front with you?"

"Sure."

"All the time?"

"Why not?"

"Well, mercy on me!"

She was Queen for a day, she thought, climbing in around him and smoothing her skirt under her as she sat down. I wonder if he knows that this is the same as having a date?

He got in on his side, got out again to tear off the streamer on a rosette that obscured his vision, then settled himself behind the wheel.

Ginger turned to smile at him. Her small face was so lighted by happiness that he didn't start his motor. He just sat and grinned back at her. He didn't see how anyone could possibly radiate so much happiness. And when she cried, "Oh, Spark Plug, isn't this *fun?*" she surprised him into an honest answer.

"Why, yeah," he said. "You bet."

He honked his horn, they sat up proudly; and Ginger's parents, and his, all rushing to their front windows to watch the take-off, saw Beauty roll along the driveway and out into the street. She did it smoothly and with a dignity befitting her age.

After nearly half a century of idle rusting, she was once again fulfilling her mechanical mission. She was carrying youth and "personality" to a football game.